TANDEM

The Man in the Maze

"Tomorrow," Boardman said, "we'll fly over the maze and map it a little, and then we'll start sending men in. I figure we'll be talking to Muller within a week."

"Do you think he'll be willing to co-operate?"

"He won't at first. He'll be so full of bitterness that he'll be spitting poison. After all, we're the ones who cast him out. Why should he want to help Earth now? But he'll come around, Ned. We'll work on Muller. We'll get him to come out of that damned maze and help us."

"But Muller's had nine years to stew in his misery," Rawlins said. "What if it's impossible to get near him now? What if the stuff he radiates is so strong that we won't be able to stand it?"

"We'll stand it," Boardman said.

Also by Robert Silverberg

THE TIME-HOPPERS   Tandem edition 5/–

HAWKSBILL STATION   Tandem edition 5/–

The Man in the Maze

Robert Silverberg

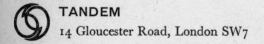
TANDEM
14 Gloucester Road, London SW7

First published in Great Britain by
Sidgwick & Jackson Ltd, 1969
Published by Universal-Tandem Publishing Co. Ltd, 1971

Made and printed in Great Britain by
The Garden City Press Ltd, Letchworth, Herts.

CHAPTER ONE

Muller knew the maze quite well by this time. He understood its snares and its delusions, its pitfalls, its deadly traps. He had lived within it for nine years. That was long enough to come to terms with the maze, if not with the situation that had driven him to take refuge within it.

He still moved warily. Three or four times already he had learned that his knowledge of the maze, although adequate and workable, was not wholly complete. At least once he had come right to the edge of destruction, pulling back only by some improbable bit of luck just before the unexpected fountaining of an energy flare sent a stream of raw power boiling across his path. Muller had charted that flare, and fifty others; but as he moved through the city-sized labyrinth he knew there was no guarantee that he would not meet an uncharted one.

Overhead the sky was darkening; the deep, rich green of late afternoon was giving way to the black of night. Muller paused a moment in his hunting to look up at the pattern of the stars. Even that was becoming familiar now. He had chosen his own constellations on this desolate world, searching the heavens for arrangements of brightness that suited his peculiar harsh and bitter taste. Now they appeared: the Dagger, the Back, the Shaft, the Ape, the Toad. In the forehead of the Ape flickered the small grubby star that Muller believed was the sun of Earth. He was not sure, because he had destroyed his chart tank after landing here. Somehow, though, he felt that that minor fireball must be Sol. The same dim star formed the left eye of the Toad. There were times when Muller told himself that Sol would not be visible in the sky of this world ninety light-years from Earth, but at other times he was quite convinced. Beyond the Toad lay the constellation that Muller had named Libra, the

5

Scales. Of course, this set of scales was badly out of balance.

Three small moons glittered here. The air was thin but breathable; Muller had long ago ceased to notice that it had too much nitrogen, not enough oxygen. It was a little short on carbon dioxide, too, and one effect of that was that he hardly ever seemed to yawn. That did not trouble him. Gripping the butt of his gun tightly, he walked slowly through the alien city in search of his dinner. This too was part of a fixed routine. He had six months' supply of food stored in a radiation locker half a kilometre away, but yet each night he went hunting so that he could replace at once whatever he drew from his cache. It was a way of devouring the time. And he needed that cache, undepleted, against the day when the maze might cripple or paralyse him. His keen eyes scanned the angled streets ahead. About him rose the walls, screens, traps and confusions of the maze within which he lived. He breathed deeply. He put each foot firmly down before lifting the other. He looked in all directions. The triple moonlight analysed and dissected his shadow, splitting it into reduplicated images that danced and sprawled before him.

The mass detector mounted over his left ear emitted a high-pitched sound. That told Muller that it had picked up the thermals of an animal in the 50-100 kilogram range. He had the detector programmed to scan in three horizons, of which this was the middle one, the food-beast range. The detector would also report to him on the proximity of 10-20 kilogram creatures—the teeth-beast range—and on the emanations of beasts over 500 kilograms—the big-beast range. The small ones had a way of going quickly for the throat, and the great ones were careless tramplers; Muller hunted those in between and avoided the others.

Now he crouched, readying his weapon. The animals that wandered the maze here on Lemnos could be slain without strategem; they kept watch on one another, but even after all the years of Muller's presence among them they had not learned that he was predatory. Not in several million years had an intelligent life-form done any hunting on this planet, evidently, and Muller had been potting them nightly without teaching them a thing about the nature of mankind. His only concern in hunting was to strike from a secure, well-surveyed point so that in his concentration on his prey he would not fall victim to some more dangerous creature. With the kickstaff mounted on the heel of his left boot he probed the wall behind him, making certain that it would not open and engulf him. It was solid. Good. Muller edged himself backward until his back touched the cool, polished stone. His left knee rested on the faintly yielding pavement. He sighted along the barrel of his gun. He was safe. He could wait. Perhaps three minutes went by. The mass detector continued to whine, indicating that the beast was remaining within a hundred-metre radius; the pitch rose slightly from moment to moment as the thermals grew stronger. Muller was in no hurry. He was at one side of a vast plaza bordered by glassy curving partitions, and anything that emerged from those gleaming crescents would be an easy shot. Muller was hunting tonight in Zone E of the maze, the fifth sector out from the heart, and one of the most dangerous. He rarely went past the relatively innocuous Zone D, but some daredevil mood had prodded him into E this evening. Since finding his way into the maze he had never risked G or H again at all, and had been as far out as F only twice. He came to E perhaps five times a year.

To his right the converging lines of a shadow appeared, jutting from one of the curving glassy walls. The song of the mass detector reached into the upper end of the pitch spectrum for an animal of this size. The smallest moon, Atropos, swinging giddily through the sky, changed the shadow pattern; the lines no longer converged, but now one bar of blackness cut across the other two. The shadow of a snout, Miller knew. An instant later he saw his victim. The animal was the size of a large dog, grey of muzzle and tawny of body, hump-shouldered, ugly, spectacularly carnivorous. For his first few years here Muller had avoided hunting the carnivores, thinking that their meat

7

would not be tasty. He had gone instead after the local equivalent of cows and sheep—mild-mannered ungulates which drifted blithely through the maze cropping the grasses in the garden places. Only when that bland meat palled did he go after one of the fanged, clawed creatures that harvested the herbivores, and to his surprise their flesh was excellent. He watched the animal emerge into the plaza. Its long snout twitched. Muller could hear the sniffing sounds from where he crouched. But the scent of man meant nothing to this beast.

Confidently, swaggeringly, the carnivore strode across the sleek pavement of the plaza, its unretracted claws clicking and scraping. Muller fined his beam down to needle aperture and took thoughtful aim, sighting now on the hump, now on the hindquarters. The gun was proximity-responsive and would score a hit automatically, but Muller always keyed in the manual sighting. He and the gun had different goals—the gun was concerned with killing, Muller with eating; and it was easier to do his own aiming than to try to convince the weapon that a bolt through the tender, juicy hump would deprive him of the tastiest cut. The gun, seeking the simplest target, would lance through that hump to the spine and bring the beast down : Muller favoured more finesse.

He chose a target six inches forward from the hump : the place where the spine entered the skull. One shot did it. The animal toppled heavily. Muller went towards it as rapidly as he dared, checking every footfall. Quickly he carved away the inessentials—limbs, head, belly—and sprayed a seal around the raw slab of flesh he cut from the hump. He sliced a hefty steak from the hindquarters, too, and strapped both parcels to his shoulders. Then he swung around, searching for the zigzagging road that was the only safe entry to the core of the maze. In less than an hour he could be at his lair in the heart of Zone A.

He was halfway across the plaza when he heard an unfamiliar sound.

Pausing, he looked back. Three small loping creatures were heading towards the carcass he had abandoned.

But the scrabbling of the scavengers was not what he had heard. Was the maze preparing some new devilry? It had been a low rumbling sound overlaid by a hoarse throb in the middle frequencies, too prolonged to be the roaring of one of the large animals. It was a sound Muller had not heard before.

No: a sound he had not heard *here* before. It registered somewhere in his memory banks. He searched. The sound was familiar. That double boom, slowly dopplering into the distance—what was it?

He placed its position. The sound had come from over his right shoulder, so it seemed. Muller looked there and saw only the triple cascade of the maze's secondary wall, rising in tier upon glittering amber tier. Above that wall? He saw the star-brightened sky: the Ape, the Toad, the Scales.

Muller remembered the sound now.

A ship; a starship, cutting out of warp on to ion drive to make a planetary landing. The boom of the expellers, the throb of the deceleration tubes, passing over the city. It was a sound he had not heard in nine years, since his self-exile on Lemnos had begun. So he was having visitors. Casual intruders, or had he been traced? What did they want? Anger blazed through him. He had had enough of them and their world. Why did they have to trouble him here? Muller stood braced, legs apart, a segment of his mind searching as always for perils even while he glared towards the probable landing point of the ship. He wanted nothing to do with Earth or Earthmen. He glowered at the faint point of light in the eye of the Toad, in the forehead of the Ape.

They would not reach him, he decided.

They would die in the maze, and their bones would join the million-year accumulation that lay strewn in the outer corridors.

And if they succeeded in entering, as he had done—

Well, then they would have to contend with him. They would not find that pleasant. Muller smiled grimly, adjusted the meat on his back, and returned his full

9

concentration to the job of penetrating the maze. Soon he was within Zone C, and safe. He reached his lair. He stowed his meat. He prepared his dinner. Pain hammered at his skull. After nine years he was no longer alone on this world. They had soiled his solitude. Once again, Muller felt betrayed. He wanted nothing more from Earth than privacy, now; and even that they would not give him. But they would suffer if they managed to reach him within the maze. If.

2

The ship had erupted from warp a little late, almost in the outer fringes of Lemnos' atmosphere. Charles Boardman disliked that. He demanded the highest possible standards of performance from himself, and expected everyone about him to keep to the same standards. Especially pilots.

Concealing his irritation, Boardman thumbed the screen to life and the cabin wall blossomed with a vivid image of the planet below. Scarcely any clouds swathed its surface; he had a clear view through the atmosphere. In the midst of a broad plain was a series of corrugations that were sharply outlined even at a height of a hundred kilometres. Boardman turned to the young man beside him and said, "There you are, Ned. The labyrinth of Lemnos. And Dick Muller right in the middle of it!"

Ned Rawlins pursed his lips. "So big? It must be hundreds of kilometres across!"

"What you're seeing is the outer embankment. The maze itself is surrounded by a concentric ring of earthen walls five metres high and nearly a thousand kilometres in outer circumference. But—"

"Yes, I know," Rawlins burst in. Almost immediately he turned bright red, with that appealing innocence that Boardman found so charming and soon would be trying to put to use. "I'm sorry, Charles, I didn't mean to interrupt."

"Quite all right. What did you want to ask?"

"That dark spot within the outer walls—is that the city itself?"

Boardman nodded. "That's the inner maze. Twenty, thirty kilometres in diameter—and God knows how many millions of years old. That's where we'll find Muller."

"If we can get inside."

"*When* we get inside."

"Yes. Yes. Of course. *When* we get inside," Rawlins corrected, reddening again. He flashed a quick, earnest smile. "There's no chance we won't find the entrance, is there?"

"Muller did," said Boardman quietly. "He's in there."

"But he's the first who got inside. Everyone else who tried has failed. So why will we—"

"There weren't many who tried," Boardman said. "Those who did weren't equipped for the problem. We'll manage, Ned. We'll manage. We have to. Relax, now, and enjoy the landing."

The ship swung towards the planet—going down much too rapidly, Boardman thought, oppressed by the strains of deceleration. He hated travel, and he hated the moment of landing worst of all. But this was a trip he could not have avoided. He eased back in the webfoam cradle and blanked out the screen. Ned Rawlins was still upright, eyes glowing with excitement. How wonderful to be young, Boardman thought, not sure whether he meant to be sarcastic or not. Certainly the boy was strong and healthy—and cleverer than he sometimes seemed. A likely lad, as they would have said a few centuries ago. Boardman could not remember having been that sort of young man himself. He had the feeling of having always been on the brink of middle-age—shrewd, calculating, well organised. He was eighty, now, with almost half his lifetime behind him, and yet in honest self-appraisal he could not bring himself to believe that his personality had changed in any essential way since he had turned twenty. He had learned techniques, the craft of managing men; he was wiser now; but he was not qualitatively different. Young Ned Rawlins, though, was going to be another person entirely sixty-odd years from now, and very little of the callow boy in the next cradle would survive. Boardman suspected, not happily, that this very mission would be the crucible in which Ned's innocence was blasted from him.

Boardman closed his eyes as the ship entered its final landing manoeuvres. He felt gravity clawing at his ageing flesh. Down. Down. Down. How many planetfalls had he made, loathing every one? The diplomatic life was a restless one. Christmas on Mars, Easter on one of the Centaurine worlds, the midyear feast celebrated on a stinking planet of Rigel—and now this trip, the most complex of all. Man was not made to flash from star to star like this, Boardman thought. I have lost my sense of a universe. They say this is the richest era of human existence; but I think a man can be richer in knowing every atom of a single golden island in a blue sea than by spending his days striding among all the worlds.

He knew that his face was distorted by the pull of Lemnos as the ship plunged planetward. There were heavy fleshy jowls about his throat, and pockets of extra meat here and there about his body, giving him a soft, pampered look. With little effort Boardman could have had himself streamlined to the fashionably sleek appearance of a modern man; this was an era when men a century and a quarter old could look like striplings, if they cared to. Early in his career Boardman had chosen to simulate his authentic ageing. Call it an investment; what he forfeited in chic he gained in status. His business was selling advice to governments, and governments preferred not to buy their counsel from men who looked like boys. Boardman had looked fifty-five years old for the last forty years, and he expected to retain that look of strong, vigorous early middle age at least another half a century. Later, he would allow time to work on him again when he entered the final phase of his career. He would take on the whitened hair and shrunken cheek of a man of eighty, and pose as Nestor rather than as Ulysses. At the moment it was professionally useful to look only slightly out of trim, as he did.

He was a short man, though he was so stocky that he easily dominated any group at a conference table. His powerful shoulders, deep chest, and long arms would have been better suited to a giant. When he stood up Boardman revealed himself as of less than middle height, but sitting down he was awesome. He found that feature useful too, and had never considered altering it. An extremely tall man is better suited to command than to advise, and Boardman had never had the wish to command; he preferred a more subtle exercise of power. But a short man who looks big at a table can control empires. The business of empires is transacted sitting down.

He had the look of authority. His chin was strong, his nose thick and blunt and forceful, his lips both firm and sensuous, his eyebrows immense and shaggy, black strips of fur sprouting from a massive forehead that might have awed a Neanderthal. He wore his hair long and coarse. Three rings gleamed on his fingers, one a gyroscope of platinum and rubies with dull-hued inlays of U-238. His taste in clothing was severe and conservative, running to heavy fabrics and almost medieval cuts. In another epoch he might have been well cast as a worldly cardinal or as an ambitious prime minister; he would have been important in any court at any time. He was important now. The price of Boardman's importance, though, was the turmoil of travel. Soon he would land on another strange planet, where the air would smell wrong, the gravity would be just a shade too strong, and the sun's hue would not be right. Boardman scowled. How much longer would the landing take?

He looked at Ned Rawlins. Twenty-two, twenty-three years old, something like that: the picture of naive young manhood, although Boardman knew that Ned was old enough to have learned more than he seemed to show. Tall, conventionally handsome without the aid of cosmetic surgery; fair hair, blue eyes, wide, mobile lips, flawless teeth. He was the son of a communications theorist, now dead, who had been one of Richard Muller's closest friends. Boardman was counting on that connection to carry them a good distance in the delicate transactions ahead.

Rawlins said, "Are you uncomfortable, Charles?"

"I'll live. We'll be down soon."

"The landing seems so slow, doesn't it?"

"Another minute now," Boardman said.

The boy's face looked scarcely stretched by the forces acting upon them. His left cheek was drawn down slightly, that was all. It was weird to see the semblance of a sneer on that shining visage.

"Here we come now," Boardman muttered, and closed his eyes again.

The ship closed the last gap between itself and the ground. The expellers cut out; the deceleration tubes snarled their last. There was the final awkward moment of uncertainty, then steadiness, the landing jacks gripping firmly, the roar of landing silenced. We are here, Boardman thought. Now for the maze. Now for Mr. Richard Muller. Now to see if he's become any less horrible in the past nine years. Maybe he's just like everyone else, by now. If he is, Boardman told himself, God help us all.

Ned Rawlins had not travelled much. He had visited only five worlds, and three of them were in the mother system. When he was ten, his father had taken him on a summer tour of Mars. Two years later he had seen Venus and Mercury. As his graduation present at sixteen he had gone extrasolar as far as Alpha Centauri IV, and three years after that he had made the melancholy trip to the Rigel system to bring home his father's body after the accident.

It wasn't much of a travel record at a time when the warp drive made getting from one cluster to another not much more difficult than going from Europe to Australia, Rawlins knew. But he had time to do his jaunting later on, when he began getting his diplomatic assignments. To hear Charles Boardman tell it, the joys of travel palled pretty fast, anyway, and running around the universe became just another chore. Rawlins made allowances for the jaded attitude of a man nearly four times his own age, but he suspected that Boardman was telling the truth.

Let the jadedness come. Right now Ned Rawlins was walking an alien world for the sixth time in his life, and he loved it. The ship was docked on the big plain that surrounded Muller's maze; the outer embankments of the maze itself lay a hundred kilometres to the southeast. It was the middle of the night on this side of Lemnos. The planet had a thirty-hour day and a twenty-month year; it was early autumn in this hemisphere, and the air was chilly. Rawlins stepped away from the ship. The crewmen were unloading the extruders that would build their camp. Charles Boardman stood to one side, wrapped in a thick fur garment and buried in an introspective mood so deep that Rawlins did not dare go near him. Rawlins' attitude towards Boardman was one of mingled awe and terror. He knew that the man was a cynical old bastard, but despite that it was impossible to feel anything but admiration for him. Boardman, Rawlins knew, was an authentic great man. He hadn't met many. His own father had been one, perhaps. Dick Muller had been another; but of course Rawlins hadn't been much more than twelve years old when Muller got into the hideous mess that had shattered his life. Well, to have known three such men in one short lifetime was a privilege indeed, Rawlins told himself. He wished that his own career would turn out half as impressively as Boardman's had. Of course he didn't have Boardman's foxiness, and hoped he never would. But he had other characteristics—a nobility of soul, in a way—which Boardman lacked. I can be of service in my own style, Rawlins thought, and then wondered if that was a naive hope.

He filled his lungs with alien air. He stared at a sky swarming with strange stars, and looked futilely for some familiar pattern. A frosty wind ripped across the plain. This planet seemed forlorn, desolate, empty. He had read about Lemnos in school : one of the abandoned ancient planets of an unknown alien race, lifeless for a thousand centuries. Nothing remained of its people except fossilized bones and shreds of artifacts—and the maze. Their deadly labyrinth ringed a city of the dead that seemed almost untouched.

Archaeologists had scanned the city from the air, probing it with sensors and curdling in frustration, unable to enter it safely. The first dozen expeditions to Lemnos had failed to find a way into the maze; every man who entered had perished, a victim of the hidden traps so cleverly planted in the outer zones. The last attempt to get inside had been made some fifty years ago. Then Richard Muller had come here, looking for a place to hide from mankind, and somehow he had found the route.

Rawlins wondered if they would succeed in making contact with Muller. He wondered, too, how many of the men he had journeyed with would die before they got into the maze. He did not consider the possibility of his own death. At his age, death was still something that happened to other people. But some of the men now working to set up their camp would be dead in a few days.

While he thought about that an animal appeared, padding out from behind a sandy hummock a short distance from him. Rawlins regarded the alien beast curiously. It looked a little like a big cat, but its claws did not retract and its mouth was full of greenish fangs. Luminous stripes gave its lean sides a gaudy hue. Rawlins could not see what use such a glowing hide would be to a predator, unless it used the radiance as a kind of bait.

The animal came within a dozen metres of Rawlins, peered at him without any sign of interest, then turned gracefully and trotted towards the ship. The combination of strange beauty, power, and menace that the animal presented was an attractive one.

It was approaching Boardman now. And Boardman was drawing a weapon.

"No!" Rawlins found himself yelling. "Don't kill it, Charles! It only wants to look at us—!"

Boardman fired.

The animal leaped, convulsed in mid-air, and fell back with its limbs outspread. Rawlins rushed up, numb with shock. There hadn't been any need for the killing, he thought. The beast was just scouting us out. What a filthy thing to do!

He blurted angrily, "Couldn't you have waited a minute, Charles? Maybe it would have gone away by itself! Why—"

Boardman smiled. He beckoned to a crewman, who squirted a spray net over the fallen animal. The beast stirred groggily as the crewman hauled it towards the ship. Softly Boardman said, "All I did was stun it, Ned. We're going to write off part of the budget for this trip against the account of the federal zoo. Did you think I was all that trigger-happy?"

Rawlins suddenly felt very small and foolish. "Well—not really. That is—"

"Forget it. No, don't forget it. Don't forget anything. Take a lesson from it: collect all the data before shouting nonsense."

"But if I had waited, and you really had killed it—"

"Then you'd have learned something ugly about me at the expense of one animal life. You'd have the useful fact that I'm provoked to murderousness by anything strange with sharp teeth. Instead all you did was make a loud noise. If I had meant to kill, your shout wouldn't have changed my intention. It might have ruined my aim, that's all, and left me at the mercy of an angry wounded beast. So bide your time, Ned. Evaluate. It's better sometimes to let a thing happen than to play your own hand too quickly." Boardman winked. "Am I offending you, Ned? Making you feel like an idiot with my little lecture?"

"Of course not, Charles. I wouldn't pretend that I don't have plenty to learn."

"And you're willing to learn it from me, even if I'm an infuriating old scoundrel?"

"Charles, I—"

"I'm sorry, Ned. I shouldn't be teasing you. You were right to stop me from killing that animal. It wasn't your fault that you misunderstood what I was doing. In your place I'd have acted just the way you did."

"You mean I shouldn't have bided my time and collected all the data when you pulled the stungun?" Rawlins asked,

17

baffled.

"Probably not."

"You're contradicting yourself, Charles."

"It's my privilege to be inconsistent," Boardman said. "My stock in trade, even." He laughed heartily. "Get a good night's sleep tonight. Tomorrow we'll fly over the maze and map it a little, and then we'll start sending men in. I figure we'll be talking to Muller within a week."

"Do you think he'll be willing to cooperate?"

A cloud passed over Boardman's heavy features. "He won't be at first. He'll be so full of bitterness that he'll be spitting poison. After all, we're the ones who cast him out. Why should he want to help Earth now? But he'll come around, Ned, because fundamentally he's a man of honour, and that's something that never changes no matter how sick and lonely and anguished a man gets. Not even hatred can corrode real honour. You know that, Ned, because you're that sort of person yourself. Even I am, in my own way. A man of honour. We'll work on Muller. We'll get him to come out of that damned maze and help us."

"I hope you're right, Charles." Rawlins hesitated. "And what will it be like for us, confronting him? I mean, considering his sickness—the way he affects others—"

"It'll be bad. Very bad."

"You saw him, didn't you, after it happened?"

"Yes. Many times."

Rawlins said, "I can't really imagine what it's like to be next to a man and feel his whole soul spilling out over you. That's what happens when you're with Muller, isn't it?"

"It's like stepping into a bath of acid," said Boardman heavily. "You can get used to it, but you never like it. You feel fire all over your skin. The ugliness, the terrors, the greeds, the sicknesses—they spout from him like a fountain of muck."

"And Muller's a man of honour ... a decent man."

"He was, yes." Boardman looked towards the distant maze. "Thank God for that. But it's a sobering thought, isn't it, Ned? If a first-rate man like Dick Muller has all that garbage inside his brain, what do you think ordinary people

18

are like in there? The squashed-down people with the squashed-down lives? Give them the same kind of curse Muller has and they'd be like beacons of flame, burning up every mind within light-years."

"But Muller's had nine years to stew in his misery," Rawlins said. "What if it's impossible to get near him now? What if the stuff he radiates is so strong that we won't be able to stand it?"

"We'll stand it," Boardman said.

CHAPTER TWO

WITHIN THE maze, Muller studied his situation and contemplated his options. In the milky green recesses of the viewing tank he could see the ship and the plastic domes that had sprouted beside it, and the tiny figures of men moving about. He wished now that he had been able to find the fine control on the viewing tank; the images he received were badly out of focus. But he considered himself lucky to have the use of the tank at all. Many of the ancient instruments in this city had become useless long ago through the decay of some vital part. A surprising number had endured the aeons unharmed, a tribute to the technical skill of their makers; but of these, Muller had been able to discover the functions of only a few, and he operated those imperfectly.

He watched the blurred figures of his fellow humans working busily and wondered what new torment they were preparing for him.

He had tried to leave no clues to his whereabouts when he fled from Earth. He had come here in a rented ship, filing a deceptive flight plan by way of Sigma Draconis. During his warp trip, of course, he had had to pass six monitor stations; but he had given each one a simulated great-circle galactic route record, carefully designed to be as misleading as possible.

A routine comparison check of all the minor stations would reveal that Muller's successive announcements of location added up to nonsense, but he had gambled that he would manage to complete his flight and vanish before they ran one of the regular checks. Evidently he had won that gamble, for no interceptor ships had come after him.

Emerging from warp in the vicinity of Lemnos, he carried out one final evasive manoeuvre by leaving his ship in a parking orbit and descending by drop-capsule. A disruptor bomb, preprogrammed, had blasted the ship to molecules and sent the fragments travelling on a billion conflicting orbits through the universe. It would take a fancy computer indeed to calculate a probably nexus of source for those! The bomb was designed to provide fifty false vectors per square metre of explosion surface, a virtual guarantee that no tracer could possibly be effective within a finite span of time. Muller needed only a very short finite span—say, sixty years. He had been close to sixty when he left Earth. Normally, he could expect at least another century of vigorous life; but, cut off from medical service, doctoring himself with a cheap diagnostat, he'd be doing well to last into his eleventh or twelfth decade. Sixty years of solitude and a peaceful, private death, that was all he asked. But now his privacy was interrupted after only nine years.

Had they really traced him somehow?

Muller decided that they had not. For one thing, he had taken every conceivable antitracking precaution. For another, they had no motive for following him. He was no fugitive who had to be brought back to justice. He was simply a man with a loathsome affliction, an abomination in the sight of his fellow mortals, and doubtless Earth felt itself well rid of him. He was a shame and a reproach to them, a welling fount of guilt and grief, a prod to the planetary conscience. The kindest thing he could do for his own kind was to remove himself from their midst, and he had done that as thoroughly as he could. They would hardly make an effort to come looking for someone so odious to them.

Who were these intruders, then?

Archaeologists, he suspected. The ruined city of Lemnos still held a magnetic, fatal fascination for them—for everyone. Muller had hoped that the risks of the maze would continue to keep men away. It had been discovered over a century earlier, but before his arrival there had been a period of many years in which Lemnos was shunned. For good reason : Muller had many times seen the corpses of those who had tried and failed to enter the maze. He himself had come here partly out of a suicidal wish to join the roster of victims, partly out of overriding curiosity to get within and solve the secret of the labyrinth, and partly out of the knowledge that if he did penetrate he was not likely to suffer many invasions of his privacy. Now he was within; but intruders had come.

They will not enter, Muller told himself.

Snugly established at the core of the maze, he had command of enough sensing devices to follow, however vaguely, the progress of any living creatures outside. Thus he could trace the wanderings from zone to zone of the animals that were his prey, and also those of the great beasts who offered danger. To a limited degree he could control the snares of the maze, which normally were nothing more than passive traps but which could be employed aggressively, under the right conditions, against some enemy. More than once Muller had dumped an elephantine carnivore into a subterranean pit as it charged inward through Zone D. He asked himself if he would use those defences against human beings if they penetrated that far, and had no answer. He did not really hate his own species; he just preferred to be left alone, in what passed for peace.

He eyed the screens. He occupied a squat hexagonal cell—apparently one of the housing units in the inner city—which was equipped with a wall of viewing tanks. It had taken him more than a year to find out which parts of the maze corresponded to the images on the screens; but by patiently posting markers he had matched the dim images to the glossy reality. The six lowest screens along the wall showed him pictures of areas in Zones A through F; the cameras, or whatever they were, swivelled through 180° arcs, enabling the hidden mysterious eyes to patrol the entire region around each of the zone entrances. Since only one entrance provided safe access to the zone within, all others being lethal, the screens effectively allowed Muller to watch the inward progress of any prowler. It did not matter what was taking place at any of the false entrances. Those who persisted there would die.

Screens seven through ten, in the upper bank, relayed images that apparently came from Zones G and H, the outermost, largest and deadliest zones of the maze. Muller had not wanted to go to the trouble of returning to those zones to check his theory in detail; he was satisfied that the screens were pickups from points in the outer zones, and it was not worth risking those zones again to find out more accurately where the pickups were mounted. As for the eleventh and twelfth screens, they obviously showed views of the plain outside the maze altogether—the plain now occupied by a newly-arrived starship from Earth.

Few of the other devices left by the ancient builders of the maze were as informative. Mounted on a dais in the centre of the city's central plaza, shielded by a crystal vault, was a twelve-sided stone the colour of ruby, in whose depths a mechanism like an intricate shutter ticked and pulsed. Muller suspected it was some sort of clock, keyed to a nuclear oscillation and sounding out the units of time its makers employed. Periodically the stone underwent temporary changes : its face turned cloudy, deepened in hue to blue or even black, swung on its mounting. Muller's careful record-keeping had not yet told him the meaning of those changes. He could not even analyse the periodicity. The metamorphoses were not random, but the pattern they followed was beyond his comprehension.

At the eight corners of the plaza were metallic spikes, smoothly tapering to heights of some twenty feet. Throughout the cycle of the year these spikes revolved, so they were calendars, it seemed, moving on hidden bearings. Muller knew that they made one complete revolution in each thirty-month turning of Lemnos about its sombre orange primary, but he suspected some deeper purpose for these gleaming pylons. Searching for it occupied much of his time.

Spaced neatly in the streets of Zone A were cages with bars hewn from an alabaster-like rock. Muller could see no way of opening these cages; yet twice during his years here he had awakened to find the bars withdrawn into the stone pavement, and the cages gaping wide. The first time they had remained open for three days; then the bars had returned to their positions while he slept, sliding into place and showing no seam where they could have parted. When the cages opened again, a few years later, Muller watched them constantly to find the secret of their mechanism. But on the fourth night he dozed just long enough to miss the closing again.

Equally mysterious was the aqueduct. Around the length of Zone B ran a closed trough, perhaps of onyx, with angular spigots placed at fifty-metre intervals. When any sort of vessel, even a cupped hand, was placed beneath a spigot it yielded pure water. But when he attempted to poke a finger into one of the spigots he found no opening, nor could he see any even while the water was coming forth; it was as though the fluid issued through a permeable plug of stone, and Muller found it hard to accept that. He welcomed the water, though.

It surprised him that so much of the city should have survived. Archaeologists had concluded, from a study of the artifacts and skeletons found on Lemnos outside the maze, that there had been no intelligent life here for upwards of a million years—perhaps five or six million. Muller was only an amateur archaeologist, but he had had enough field experience to know the effects of the passing of time. The fossils in the plain were clearly ancient, and the stratification of the city's outer walls showed that the labyrinth was contemporary with those fossils.

Yet most of the city, supposedly built before the evolution of mankind on Earth, appeared untouched by the ages. The dry weather could account in part for that; there were no storms here, and rain had not fallen since Muller's arrival. But wind and wind-blown sand could carve walls and pavements over a million years, and there was no sign of such carving here. Nor had sand accumulated in the open streets of the city. Muller knew why. Hidden pumps collected all debris, keeping everything spotless. He had gathered handfuls of soil from the garden plots, scattering little trails here and there. Within minutes the driblets of soil had begun to slither across the polished pavement, vanishing into slots that opened briefly and closed again at the intersection of buildings and ground.

Evidently beneath the city lay a network of inconceivable machinery—imperishable caretaker devices that guarded the city against the tooth of time. Muller had not been able to reach that network, though. He lacked the equipment for breaching the pavement; it seemed invulnerable at all points. With improvised tools he had begun to dig in the garden areas, hoping to reach the subcity that way, but though he had driven one pit more than a dozen feet and another even deeper he had come upon no signs of anything below but more soil. The hidden guardians had to be there, however : the instruments that operated the viewing tanks, swept the streets, repaired the masonry, and controlled the murderous traps that studded the outer zones of the labyrinth.

It was hard to imagine a race that could build a city of this sort—a city designed to last millions of years. It was harder still to imagine how they could have vanished. Assuming that the fossils found in the burial yards outside the walls were those of the builders—not necessarily a safe assumption —this city had been put together by burly humanoids a metre and a half tall, immensely thick through the chest and shoulders, with long cunning fingers, eight to the hand, and short double-jointed legs.

They were gone from the known worlds of the universe, and nothing like them had been found in any other system; perhaps they had withdrawn to some far galaxy yet unvisited by man. Or, possibly, they had been a non-spacegoing race that evolved and perished right here on Lemnos, leaving this city as their only monument.

The rest of the planet was without trace of habitation although burial grounds had been discovered in a diminishing series radiating outward a thousand kilometres from the maze. Maybe the years had eroded all their cities except this one. Maybe this, which could have sheltered perhaps a million beings, had been their only city. There was no clue to their disappearance. The devilish ingenuity of the maze argued that in their last days they had been harassed by enemies and had retreated within this tricky fortress; but Muller knew that this hypothesis too was a speculation. For all he was aware, the maze represented nothing more than an outburst of cultural paranoia and had no relation to the actual existence of an external threat.

Had they been invaded by beings for whom the maze

posed no problems, and had they been slaughtered in their own sleek streets, and had the mechanical wardens swept away the bones? No way of knowing. They were gone. Muller, entering their city, had found it silent, desolate, as if it had never sheltered life; an automatic city, sterile, flawless. Only beasts occupied it. They had had a million years to find their way through the maze and take possession. Muller had counted some two dozen species of mammals in all sizes from rat-equivalent to elephant-equivalent. There were grazers who munched on the city's gardens, and hunters who fed on the herbivores, and the ecological balance seemed perfect. The city in the maze was like unto Isaiah's Babylon : wild beasts of the desert shall lie there; and their houses shall be full of doleful creatures; and owls shall dwell there, and satyrs shall dance there.

The city was his now. He had the rest of his lifetime to probe its mysteries.

There had been others who had come here, and not all of them had been human. Entering the maze, Muller had been treated to the sight of those who had failed to go the route. He had sighted a score of human skeletons in Zones H, G, and F. Three men had made it to E, and one to D. Muller had expected to see their bones; but what took him off guard was the collection of alien bones. In H and G he had seen the remains of great dragon-like creatures, still clad in the shreds of spacesuits. Some day curiosity might triumph over fear and he might go back out there for a second look at them. Closer to the core lay an assortment of life-forms, mostly humanoid but veering from the standard structure. How long ago they had come here, Muller could not guess; even in this dry climate, would exposed skeletons last more than a few centuries? The galactic litter was a sobering reminder of something Muller already adequately knew : that despite the experience of man's first two centuries of extrasolar travel, in which no living intelligent alien race was encountered, the universe was full of other forms of life, and sooner or later man would meet them. The boneyard on Lemnos contained relics of at least a dozen different races. It flattered Muller's ego to know that he alone, apparently, had reached

26

the heart of the maze; but it did not cheer him to think of the diversity of peoples in the universe. He had already had his fill of galactics.

The inconsistency of finding the litter of bones within the maze did not strike him for several years. The mechanisms of the city, he knew, cleaned relentlessly, tidying up everything from particles of dust to the bones of the animals on whom he fed. Yet the skeletons of would-be invaders of the maze were allowed to remain where they lay. Why the violation of neatness? Why cart away the corpse of a dead elephant-like beast that had blundered into a power snare, and leave the remains of a dead dragon killed by the same snare? Because the dragon wore protective clothing, and so was sapient? Sapient corpses were deliberately allowed to remain, Muller realized.

As warnings. ABANDON ALL HOPE, YE WHO ENTER HERE.

Those skeletons were part of the psychological warfare waged against all intruders by this mindless, deathless, diabolical city. They were reminders of the perils that lurked everywhere. How the guardian drew the subtle distinction between bodies that should be left in situ and those that should be swept away, Muller did not know; but he was convinced that the distinction was real.

He watched his screens. He eyed the tiny figures moving about the ship on the plain.

Let them come in, he thought. The city hasn't had a victim in years. It'll take care of them. I'm safe where I am.

And, he knew, that even if by some miracle they managed to reach him, they would not remain long. His own special malady would drive them away. They might be clever enough to defeat the maze, but they could not endure the affliction that made Richard Muller intolerable to his own species.

"Go away," Muller said aloud.

He heard the whirr of rotors, and stepped from his dwelling to see a dark shadow traverse the plaza. They were scouting the maze from the air. Quickly he went indoors, then smiled at his own impulse to hide. They could detect him,

of course, wherever he was. Their screens would tell them
that a human being inhabited the labyrinth. And then,
naturally, they would in their astonishment try to make
contact with him although they would not be aware of his
identity. After that—

Muller stiffened as a sudden overwhelming desire blazed
through him. To have them come to him. To talk to men
again. To break his isolation.

He *wanted* them here.

Only for an instant. After the momentary breakthrough
of loneliness came the return of rationality—the chilling
awareness of what it would be like to face his kind again. No,
he thought. Keep out! Or die in the maze. Keep out. Keep
out. Keep out.

2

"Right down there," Boardman said. "That's where he must
be, eh, Ned? You can see the glow on the face of the tank.
We're picking up the right mass, the right density, the right
everything. One live man, and it's got to be Muller."

"At the heart of the maze," said Rawlins. "So he really
did it!"

"Somehow." Boardman peered into the viewing tank.
From a height of a couple of kilometres the structure of the
inner city was clear. He could make out eight distinct zones,
each with its characteristic style of architecture; its plazas
and promenades; its angling walls; its tangle of streets swirl-
ing in dizzyingly alien patterns. The zones were concentric,
fanning out from a broad plaza at the heart of it all, and the
scoutplane's mass detector had located Muller in a row of
low buildings just to the east of the plaza. What Boardman
failed to make out was any obvious passage linking zone to
zone. There was no shortage of blind alleys, but even from
the air the true route was not apparent; what was it like
trying to work inward on the ground?

It was all but impossible, Boardman knew. The master
data banks in the ship held the accounts of those early
explorers who had tried it and failed. Boardman had brought

with him every scrap of information on the penetration of the maze, and none of it was very encouraging except the one puzzling but incontrovertible datum that Richard Muller had managed to get inside.

Rawlins said, "This is going to sound naïve, I know, Charles. But why don't we just come down from here and land the scoutplane in the middle of that central plaza?"

"Let me show you," said Boardman.

He spoke a command. A robot drone probe detached itself from the belly of the plane and streaked towards the city. Boardman and Rawlins followed the flight of the blunt grey metal projectile until it was only a few score metres above the tops of the buildings. Through its faceted eye they had a sharp view of the city, revealing the intricate texture of much of the stonework. Suddenly the drone probe vanished. There was a burst of incandescence, a puff of greenish smoke— and then nothing at all.

Boardman nodded. "Nothing's changed. There's still a protective field over the whole thing. It volatilizes anything that tries to get through."

"So even a bird that comes too close—"

"There are no birds on Lemnos."

"Raindrops, then. Whatever falls on the city—"

"Lemnos gets no rain," said Boardman sourly. "At least not on this continent. The only thing that field keeps out is strangers. We've known it since the first expedition. Some brave men found out about that field the hard way."

"Didn't they try a drone probe first?"

Smiling, Boardman said, "When you find a dead city in the middle of a desert on a dead world you don't expect to be blown up if you land inside it. It's a forgivable sort of mistake—except that Lemnos doesn't forgive mistakes." He gestured, and the plane dropped lower, following the orbit of the outer walls for a moment. Then it rose and hovered over the heart of the city while photographs were being taken. The wrong-coloured sunlight glistened off a hall of mirrors. Boardman felt curdled weariness in his chest. They overflew the city again and again, marking off a pre-programmed observation pattern, and he discovered he was wishing irritably that a shaft of sudden light would rise from those mirrors and incinerate them on the next pass to save him the trouble of carrying out this assignment. He had lost his taste for detail work, and too many fine details stood between him and his purpose here. They said that impatience was a mark of youth, that old men could craftily spin their webs and plot their schemes in serenity, but somehow Boardman found himself longing rashly for a quick consummation to this job. Send some sort of drone scuttling through the maze on metal tracks to seize Muller and drag him out. Tell the man what was wanted of him and make him agree to do it. Then take off for Earth, quickly, quickly. The mood passed. Boardman felt foxy again.

Captain Hosteen, who would be conducting the actual entry attempt, came aft to pay his respects. Hosteen was a short, thick-framed man with a flat nose and coppery skin; he wore his uniform as though he felt it was all going to slip off his left shoulder at any moment. But he was a good man, Boardman knew, and ready to sacrifice a score of lives, including his own, to get into that maze.

Hosteen flicked a glance from the screen to Boardman's face and said, "Learning anything?"

"Nothing new. We have a job."

"Want to go down again?"

"Might as well," Boardman said. He looked at Rawlins. "Unless you have anything else you'd like to check, Ned?"

"Me? Oh, no—no. That is—well, I wonder if we need to go into the maze at all. I mean, if we could lure Muller out somehow, talk to him outside the city—"

"No."

"Wouldn't it work?"

"No," said Boardman emphatically. "Item one, Muller wouldn't come out if we asked him. He's a misanthrope. Remember? He buried himself here to get away from humanity. Why should he socialize with us? Item two, we couldn't invite him outside without letting him know too much about what we want from him. In this deal, Ned, we need to hoard our resources of strategy, not toss them away in our first move."

"I don't understand what you mean."

Patiently Boardman said, "Suppose we used your approach. What would you say to Muller to make him come out?"

"Why—that we're here from Earth to ask him if he'll help us in a time of system-wide crisis. That we've encountered a race of alien beings with whom we're unable to communicate, and that it's absolutely necessary that we break through to them in a hurry, and that he alone can do the trick. We—" Rawlins stopped, as though the fatuity of his own words had broken through to him. Colour mounted in his cheeks. He said in a hoarse voice, "Muller isn't going to give a damn for those arguments, is he?"

"No, Ned. Earth sent him before a bunch of aliens once before, and they ruined him. He isn't about to try it again."

"Then how are we going to make him help us?"

"By playing on his sense of honour. But at the moment that's not the problem we're talking about. We're discussing how to get him out of his sanctuary in there. Now, you were suggesting that we set up a speaker and tell him exactly what we want from him, and then wait for him to waltz out and pledge to do his best for good old Earth. Right?"

"I guess so."

"But it won't work. Therefore we've got to get inside the maze ourselves, win Muller's trust, and persuade him to cooperate. And to do that we have to keep quiet about the real situation until we've eased him out of his suspicions."

A look of newborn wariness appeared on Rawlins' face. "What are we going to tell him, then, Charles?"

"Not *we*. You."

"What am I going to tell him, then?"

Boardman sighed. "Lies, Ned. A pack of lies."

3

They had come equipped for solving the problem of the maze. The ship's brain, of course, was a first-class computer, and it carried the details of all previous Earth-based attempts to enter the city. Except one, and unfortunately that had been the only successful one. But records of past failures have their uses. The ship's data banks had plenty of mobile extensions : airborne and groundborne drone probes, spy-eyes, sensor batteries, and more. Before any human life was risked on the maze Boardman and Hosteen would try the whole mechanical array. Mechanicals were expendable, anyway; the ship carried a set of templates, and it would be no trouble to replicate all devices destroyed. But a point would come at which the drone probes had to give way to men : the aim was to gather as much information as possible for those men to use.

Never before had anyone tried to crack the maze this way. The early explorers had simply gone walking in, unsuspecting, and had perished. Their successors had known enough of the story to avoid the more obvious traps, and to some extent had been aided by sophisticated sensory devices, but this was the first attempt to run a detailed survey before entering. No one was overly confident that the technique would let them in unscathed, but it was the best way to approach the problem.

The overflights on the first day had given everybody a good visual image of the maze. Strictly speaking, it hadn't been necessary for them to leave the ground; they could have watched big-screen relays from the comfort of their camp and gained a decent idea of the conformation below, letting airborne probes do all the work. But Boardman had insisted. The mind registers things one way when it picks them off a relay screen, and another when the sensory impressions are flooding in straight from the source. Now they all had seen the city from the air, and had seen what the guardians of the maze could do to a drone probe that ventured into the protective field overlying the city.

Rawlins had suggested the possibility that there might be a null spot in that protective field. Towards late afternoon they checked it out by loading a probe with metal pellets and stationing it fifty metres above the highest point of the maze. Scanner eyes recorded the action as the drone slowly turned, spewing the pellets one at a time into preselected one-square-metre boxes above the city. Each in turn was incinerated as it fell. They were able to calculate that the thickness of the safety field varied with distance from the centre of the maze; it was only about two metres deep above the inner zones, much deeper at the outer rim, forming an invisible cup over the city. But there were no null spots; the field was continuous. Hosteen tested the notion that the field was capable of overstrain by having the probe reloaded with pellets which were catapulted simultaneously into each of the test rectangles. The field dealt with them all, creating for a moment a single pucker of flame above the city.

At the expense of a few mole probes they found out that reaching the city through a tunnel was equally impossible. The moles burrowed into the coarse sandy soil outside the outer walls, chewed themselves passageways fifty metres down, and nosed upwards again when they were beneath the maze. They were destroyed by the safety field while still twenty metres below ground level. A try at burrowing in right at the base of the embankments also failed; the field went straight down, apparently, all around the city.

A power technician offered to rig an interference pylon to drain the energy of the field. It didn't work. The pylon, a hundred metres tall, sucked in power from all over the planet; blue lightning leaped and hissed along its accumulator bank, but it had no effect on the safety field. They reversed the pylon and sent a million kilowatts shooting into the city, hoping to short the field. The field drank everything and seemed ready for more. No one had any rational theory to explain the field's power source. "It must tap the planet's own energy of rotation," the technician who had rigged the pylon said, and then, realizing he hadn't contributed anything useful, he looked away and began to snap orders into the handmike he carried.

Three days of similar researches demonstrated that the city was invulnerable to intrusion from above or below.

"There's only one way in," said Hosteen, "and that's on foot, through the main gate."

"If the people in the city really wanted to be safe," Rawlins asked, "Why did they leave even a gate open?"

"Maybe they wanted to go in and out themselves, Ned,"

said Boardman quietly. "Or maybe they wanted to give invaders a sporting chance. Hosteen, shall we send some probes inside?"

The morning was grey. Clouds the colour of wood smoke stained the sky; it looked almost as if rain were on the way. A harsh wind knifed the soil from the plain and sent it slicing into their faces. Behind the veil of clouds lay the sun, a flat orange disc that seemed to have been pasted into the sky. It seemed only slightly larger than Sol as seen from Earth, though it was less than half as distant. Lemnos' sun was a gloomy M dwarf, cool and weary, an old star circled by a dozen old planets. Lemnos, the innermost, was the only one that had ever sustained life; the others were frigid and dead, beyond the range of the sun's feeble rays, frozen from core to atmosphere. It was a sleepy system with so little angular momentum that even the innermost planet dawdled along in a thirty-month orbit; the three zippy moons of Lemnos, darting or crisscrossing tracks a few thousand kilometres overhead, were flagrantly out of keeping with the prevailing mood of these worlds.

Ned Rawlins felt a chill at his heart as he stood beside the data terminal a thousand metres from the outer embankment of the maze, watching his shipmates marshalling their probes and instruments. Not even dead pockmarked Mars had depressed him like this, for Mars was a world that had never lived at all, while here life had been and had moved onward. This world was a house of the dead. In Thebes, once, he had entered the tomb of Pharaoh's vizier, five thousand years gone, and while the others in his group had eyed the gay murals with their glowing scenes of white-garbed figures punting on the Nile, he had looked towards the cool stone floor where a dead beetle lay, clawed feet upraised on a tiny mound of dust. For him Egypt would always be that stiffened beetle in the dust; for him Lemnos was likely to be autumn winds and scoured plains and a silent city. He wondered how anyone as gifted, as full of life and energy and human warmth as Dick Muller, could ever have been willing to maroon himself inside that dismal maze.

Then he remembered what had happened to Muller on

34

Beta Hydri IV, and conceded that even a man like Muller might very well have good reasons for coming to rest on a world like this, in a city like this. Lemnos offered the perfect escape : an Earthlike world, uninhabited, where he was almost guaranteed freedom from human company. And we're here to flush him out and drag him away. Rawlins scowled. Dirty dirty dirty, he thought. The old thing about the ends and the means. Across the way Rawlins could see the blocky figure of Charles Boardman standing in front of the big data terminal, waving his arms this way and that to direct the men fanning out near the walls of the city. He began to understand that he had let Boardman dragoon him into a nasty adventure. The glib old devil hadn't gone into details, back on Earth, about the exact methods by which they were going to win Muller's co-operation. Boardman had made it sound like some kind of shining crusade. Instead it was going to be a dirty trick. Boardman never went into the details of anything before he had to, as Rawlins was beginning to see. Rule one : hoard your resources of strategy. Never tip your hand. And so here I am, part of the conspiracy.

Hosteen and Boardman had deployed a dozen drones at the various entrances to the inner part of the maze. It was already clear that the only safe way into the city was through the northeastern gate; but they had drones to spare, and they wanted all the data they could gather. The terminal Rawlins was watching flashed a partial diagram of the maze on the screen—the section immediately in front of him—and gave him a good long time to study its loops and coils, its zigzags and twists. It was his special responsibility to follow the progress of the drone through this sector. Each of the other drones was being monitored both by computer and by human observer, while Boardman and Hosteen were at the master terminal watching the progress of the entire operation all at once.

"Send them in," Boardman said.

Hosteen gave the command, and the drones rolled forward through the city's gates. Looking now through the eyes of the squat mobile probe. Rawlins got his first view of what lay in Zone H of the maze. He saw a scalloped wall of what looked like puckered blue porcelain undulating away to the left, and a barrier of metallic threads dangling from a thick stone slab to the other side. The drone skirted the threads, which tinkled and quivered in delicate response to the disturbance of the thin air; it moved to the base of the porcelain wall, and followed it at an inward-sloping angle for perhaps twenty metres. There the wall curved abruptly back on itself, forming a sort of chamber open at the top. The last time anyone had entered the maze this way—on the fourth expedition—two men had passed that open chamber; one had remained outside and was destroyed, the other had gone inside and was spared. The drone entered the chamber. A moment later a beam of pure red light lanced from the centre of a mosaic decoration on the wall and swept over the area immediately outside the chamber.

Boardman's voice came to Rawlins through the speaker taped to his ear. "We lost four of the probes the moment they went through their gates. That's exactly as expected. How's yours doing?"

"Following the plan," said Rawlins. "So far, it's okay."

"You ought to lose it within six minutes of entry. What's your elapsed time now?"

"Two minutes fifteen."

The drone was out of the chamber now and shuttling quickly through the place where the light-beam had flashed. Rawlins keyed in olfactory and got the smell of scorched air, lots of ozone. The path divided ahead. To one side was a single-span bridge of stone, arching over what looked like a pit of flame; to the other was a jumbled pile of cyclopean blocks resting precariously edge to edge. The bridge seemed far more inviting, but the drone immediately turned away from it and began to pick its way over the jumbled blocks. Rawlins asked it why, and it relayed the information that the "bridge" wasn't there at all; it was a projection beamed from scanners mounted beneath the facing piers. Requesting a simulation of an approach anyway, Rawlins got a picture of the probe walking out on to the pier and stepping unsuspectingly through the solid-looking bridge to lose its balance; and as the simulated probe struggled to regain its equilibrium, the pier tipped forward and shucked it into the fiery pit. Cute, Rawlins thought, and shuddered.

Meanwhile the real probe had clambered over the blocks and was coming down the other side, unharmed. Three minutes and eight seconds had gone by. A stretch of straight road here turned out to be as safe as it looked. It was flanked on both sides by windowless towers a hundred metres high, made of some iridescent mineral, sleek and oily-surfaced, that flashed shimmering moire patterns as the drone hurried along. At the beginning of the fourth minute the probe skirted bright grillwork like interlocking teeth, and side-stepped an umbrella-shaped piledriver that descended with crushing force. Eighty seconds later it stepped around a tiltblock that opened into a yawning abyss, deftly eluded a quintet of tetrahedal blades that sheared upwards out of the pavement, and emerged on to a sliding walkway that carried it quickly forward for exactly forty seconds more.

All this had been traversed long ago by a Terran explorer named Cartissant, since deceased. He had dictated a detailed record of his experiences within the maze. He had lasted five minutes and thirty seconds, and his mistake had come in not getting off the walkway by the forty-first second. Those who had been monitoring him outside, back then, could not say what had happened to him after that.

As his drone left the walkway, Rawlins asked for another simulation and saw a quick dramatization of the computer's best guess : the walkway opened to engulf its passenger at that point. The probe, meanwhile, was going swiftly towards what looked like the exit from this outermost zone of the maze. Beyond lay a well-lit, cheerful-looking plaza ringed with drifting blobs of a pearly glowing substance.

Rawlins said, "I'm into the seventh minute, and we're still going, Charles. There seems to be a door into Zone G just ahead. Maybe you ought to cut in and monitor my screen."

"If you lasted two more minutes, I will," Boardman said.

The probe paused just outside the inner gate. Warily it switched on its gravitron and accumulated a ball of energy with a mass equivalent to its own. It thrust the energy ball through the doorway. Nothing happened. The probe, satisfied, trundled towards the door itself. As it passed through, the sides of the door abruptly crashed together like the jaws of a mighty press, destroying the probe. Rawlins' screen went dark. Quickly he cut in one of the overhead probes; it beamed him a shot of his probe lying on the far side of the door, flattened into a two-dimensional mock-up of itself. A human being caught in that same trap would have been crushed to powder, Rawlins realized.

"My probe's been knocked out," he reported to Boardman. "Six minutes and forty seconds."

"As expected," came the reply. "We've got only two probes left. Switch over and watch."

The master diagram appeared on Rawlins' screen: a simplified and stylized light-pen picture of the entire maze as viewed from above. A small X had been placed wherever a probe had been destroyed. Rawlins found after some searching, the path his own drone had taken, with the X marked between the zone boundaries at the place of the clashing door. It seemed to him that the drone had penetrated farther than most of the others, but he had to smile at the childish pride the discovery brought him. Anyhow, two of the probes were still moving inward. One was actually inside the second zone of the maze, and the other was cruising through a passageway that gave access to that inner ring.

The diagram vanished and Rawlins saw the maze as it looked through the pickup of one of the drones. Almost daintily, the man-high pillar of metal made its way through the baroque intricacies of the maze, past a golden pillar that beamed a twanging melody in a strange key, past a pool of light, past a web of glittering metal spokes, past spiky heaps of bleached bones. Rawlins had only glancing views of the bones as the drone moved on, but he was sure that few were human relics. This place was a galactic graveyard for the bold.

Excitement built in him as the probe went on and on. He was so thoroughly wedded to it now that it was as if he were inside the maze, avoiding one deathtrap after another, and he felt a sense of triumph as minutes mounted. Fourteen had elapsed now. This second level of the maze was not so cluttered as the first; there were spacious avenues here, handsome colonnades, long radiating passages leading from the main path. He relaxed; he felt pride in the drone's agility and in the keenness of its sensory devices. The shock was immense and stinging when a paving-block upended itself unexpectedly and dumped the probe down a long chute to a place where the gears of a giant mill turned eagerly.

They had not expected that probe to get so far, anyway. The probe the others were watching was the one that had come in via the main gate—the safe gate. The slim fund of information accumulated at the price of many lives had guided that probe past all its perils, and now it was well within Zone G, and almost to the edge of F. Thus far, everything had gone as expected; the drone's experiences had matched those of them who had tackled this route on earlier expeditions. It followed their way exactly, turning here, dodging there, and it was eighteen minutes into the maze without incident.

"All right," Boardman said. "This is where Mortenson died, isn't it?"

"Yes," Hosteen answered. "The last thing he said was that he was standing by that little pyramid, and then he was cut off."

"This is where we start gaining new information, then. All we've learned so far is that our records are accurate. This is the way in. But from here on—"

The probe, lacking a guidance pattern, now moved much more slowly, hesitating at every step to extend its network of data-gathering devices in all directions. It looked for hidden doors, for concealed openings in the pavement, for projectors, lasers, mass-detectors, power sources. It fed back to the central data banks all that it learned, thus adding to the store of information with each centimetre conquered.

It conquered, altogether, twenty-three metres. As the probe passed the small pyramid it scanned the broken body of the explorer Mortenson, lost at this point 72 years earlier. It relayed the news that Mortenson had been seized by a pressure-sensitive mangle activated by an unwary footstep too close to the pyramid. Beyond, it avoided two minor traps

39

before failing to safeguard itself from a distortion screen that baffled its sensors and left it vulnerable to the descent of a pulverizing piston.

"The next one through will have to cut off all its inputs until it's past that point," Hosteen muttered. "Running through blindfolded—well, we'll manage."

"Maybe a man would do better than a machine there," said Boardman. "We don't know if that screen would muddle a man the way it did a batch of sensors."

"We're not yet ready to run a man in there," Hosteen pointed out.

Boardman agreed—none too graciously, Rawlins thought, listening to the interchange. The screen brightened again; a new drone probe was coming through. Hosteen had ordered a second wave of the machines to pick through the labyrinth, following what was now known to be the one safe access route, and several of them were at the eighteen-minute point where the deadly pyramid was located. Hosteen sent one ahead, and posted the others to keep watch. The lead probe came within range of the distortion screen and cut out its sensors; it heaved tipsily for a moment, lacking any way to get its bearings, but in a moment it was stable. It was deprived now of contact with its surroundings, and so it paid no heed to the siren song of the distortion screen, which had misled its predecessor into coming within range of the pulverizing piston. The phalanx of drones watching the scene was all outside the reach of the distorter's mischief, and fed a clear, true picture to the computer, which matched it with the fatal path of the last probe and plotted a route that skirted the dangerous piston. Moments later the blind probe began to move, guided now by inner impulses. Lacking all environmental feedback it was entirely a captive of the computer, which nudged it along in a series of tiny prods until it was safely around the hazard. On the far side, the sensors were switched on again. To check the procedure, Hosteen sent a second drone through, likewise blinded and moving entirely on internal guidance. It made it. Then he tried a third probe with its sensors on and under the influence of the distortion screen. The computer attempted to direct it along the safe path, but the probe, bedevilled by the faulty information coming through the distorter, tugged itself furiously to the side and was smashed.

"All right," Hosteen said. "If we can get a machine past it, we can get a man past it. He closes his eyes, and the computer calculates his motions step by step. We'll manage."

The lead probe began to move again. It got seventeen metres past the place of the distorter before it was nailed by a silvery grillwork that abruptly thrust up a pair of electrodes and cut loose with a bath of flame. Rawlins watched bleakly as the next probe avoided that obstacle and shortly fell victim to another. Plenty of probes waited patiently for their turn to press forward.

And soon men will be going in there too, Rawlins thought. *We'll* be going in there.

He shut off his data terminal and walked across to Boardman.

"How does it look so far?" he asked.

"Rough, but not impossible," Boardman said. "It can't be this tough all the way in."

"And if it is?"

"We won't run out of probes. We'll chart the whole maze until we know where all the danger points are, and then we'll start trying it ourselves."

Rawlins said, "Are *you* going to go in there, Charles?"

"Of course. So are you."

"With what odds on coming out?"

"Good ones," said Boardman. "Otherwise I doubt that I'd tackle it. Oh, it's a dangerous trip, Ned, but don't overestimate it. We've just begun to test that maze. We'll know it well enough in a few days more."

Rawlins considered that a moment. "Muller didn't have any probes," he said finally. "How did he survive that stuff?"

"I'm not sure," Boardman murmured. "I suppose he's just a naturally lucky man."

CHAPTER THREE

WITHIN THE maze Muller watched the proceedings on his dim screens. They were sending some sort of robots in, he saw. The robots were getting chewed up quite badly, but each successive wave of them seemed to reach deeper into the labyrinth. Trial and error had led the intruders to the correct route through Zone H and well onward into G. Muller was prepared to defend himself if the robots reached the inner zones. Meanwhile he remained calm at the centre of it all, going about his daily pursuits.

In the morning he spent a good deal of the time thinking over his past. There had been other worlds in other years, springtimes, warmer seasons than this; soft eyes looking into his eyes, hands against his hands, smiles, laughter, shining floors, and elegant figures moving through arched doorways. He had married twice. Both times the arrangements had been terminated peacefully after a decent span of years. He had travelled widely. He had dealt with ministers and kings. In his nostrils was the scent of a hundred planets strung across the sky. We make only a small blaze, and then we go out; but in his springtime and his summer he had burned brightly enough, and he did not feel he had earned this sullen, joyless autumn.

The city took care of him, after its fashion. He had a place to dwell—thousands of places; he moved from time to time for the sake of changing the view. All the houses were empty boxes. He had made a bed for himself of animal hides stuffed with scraped fur; he had fashioned a chair from sinews and skin; he needed little else. The city gave him water. Wild animals roamed here in such quantity that he would never lack for food so long as he was strong enough to hunt. From Earth he had brought with him certain basic items. He had three cubes of books and one of music; they made a stack less than a metre high and could nourish his soul for all the years

42

that remained to him. He had some woman cubes. He had a small recorder into which he sometimes dictated memoirs. He had a sketchpad. He had weapons and a mass detector. He had a diagnostat with a regenerating medical supply. It was enough.

He ate regularly. He slept well. He had no quarrels with his conscience. He had come almost to be content with his fate. One nurses bitterness only so long before one grows a cyst around the place from which the poison spews.

He blamed no one now for what had happened to him. His own hungers had brought him to this. He had tried to devour the universe; he had aspired to the condition of a god; and some implacable guiding force had hurled him down from his high place, hurled him down and smashed him, left him to crawl off to this dead world to knit his broken soul as best he could.

The way stations on his journey to this place were well known to him. At eighteen, lying naked under the stars with warmth against him, he had boasted of his lofty ambitions. At twenty-five he had begun to realize them. Before he was forty he had visited a hundred worlds, and was famous in thirty systems. A decade later he had had his delusions of statesmanship. And at the age of fifty-three he had let Charles Boardman talk him into undertaking the mission to Beta Hydri IV.

That year he was on holiday in the Tau Ceti system, a dozen light-years from home. Marduk, the fourth world, had been designed as a pleasure planet for the mining men who were engaged in stripping her sister worlds of a fortune in reactive metals. Muller had no liking for the way those planets were being plundered, but that did not prevent him from seeking relaxation on Marduk. It was nearly a season-less world, which rode upright in its orbital plane; four continents of unending springtime bathed by a tranquil shallow sea. The sea was green, the land vegetation had a faint bluish tinge, and the air had a little of the sparkle of young champagne. They had somehow made the planet into a counterfeit of Earth—Earth as it might have been in a more innocent time—all parks and meadows and cheery inns; it was a restful world whose challenges were purely synthetic. The giant fish in the seas always wearied and let themselves be played. The snow-capped mountains looked treacherous, even for climbers in gravitron boots, but no one had been lost on them yet. The beasts with which the forests were stocked were tall at the withers and snorted as they charged, but they were not as fierce as they looked. In principle, Muller disapproved of such places. But he had had enough adventures for a while, and he had come to Marduk for a few weeks of phony peace, accompanied by a girl he had met the year before and twenty light-years away.

Her name was Marta. She was tall, slim, with large dark eyes fashionably rimmed with red, and lustrous blue hair that brushed her smooth shoulders. She looked about twenty, but of course she might just as well have been ninety and on her third shape-up; you never could tell about anyone, and especially not about a woman. But somehow Muller suspected that she was genuinely young. It wasn't her litheness, her coltish agility—those are commodities that can be purchased—but some subtle quality of enthusiasm, of true girlishness that, he liked to think, was no surgical product. Whether power-swimming or tree-floating or blowdart hunting or making love, Marta seemed so totally engaged in her pleasures that they surely were relatively new to her.

Muller did not care to investigate such things too deeply. She was wealthy, Earthborn, had no visible family ties, and went where she pleased. On a sudden impulse he had phoned her and asked her to meet him on Marduk; and she had come willingly, no questions asked. She was not awed to be sharing a hotel suite with Richard Muller. Clearly she knew who he was, but the aura of fame that surrounded him was unimportant to her. What mattered was what he said to her, how he held her, what they did together; and not the accomplishments he had accumulated at other times.

They stayed at a hotel that was a spire of brilliance a thousand metres high, thrusting needle-straight out of a valley overlooking a glassy oval lake. Their rooms were two hundred floors up, and they dined in a rooftop eyrie reached by gravitron disc, and during the day all the pleasures of

44

Marduk lay spread out before them. He was with her for a week, uninterrupted. The weather was perfect. Her small cool breasts fit nicely into his cupped palms; her long slender legs encircled him pleasantly, and at the highest moments she drove her heels into his calves with sudden delicious fervour. On the eighth day Charles Boardman arrived on Marduk, hired a suite half a continent away, and invited Muller to pay a call on him.

"I'm on vacation," Muller told him.

"Give me half a day of it."

"I'm not alone, Charles."

"I know that. Bring her along. We'll take a ride. It's an important matter."

"I came here to escape important matters."

"There's never any escape, Dick. You know that. You are what you are, and we need you. Will you come?"

"Damn you," Muller said mildly.

In the morning he and Marta flew by quickboat to Board-man's hotel. Muller remembered the journey as vividly as though it had taken place last month and not almost fifteen years before. They soared above the continental divide, skimming the snowy summits of the mountains by so slim a margin that they could see the magnificent long-horned figure of a goatish rock-skipper capering across the gleaming rivers of ice : two metric tons of muscle and bone, an improbable colossus of the peaks, the costliest prey Marduk had to offer. Some men did not earn in a lifetime what it cost to buy a license to hunt rock-skipper. To Muller it seemed that even that price was too low.

They circled the mighty beast three times and streaked off into the lake country, the lowlands beyond the mountain range where a chain of diamond-bright pools girdled the fat waist of the continent, and by midday they were landed at the edge of a velvety forest of evergreens. Boardman had rented the hotel's master suite, all screens and trickery. He grasped Muller's wrist in salute, and embraced Marta with unabashed lechery. She seemed distant and restrained in Boardman's arms; quite obviously she regarded the visit as so much time lost.

"Are you hungry?" Boardman asked. "Lunch first, talk later!"

He served drinks in his suite : an amber wine out of goblets made from blue rock crystal mined on Ganymede. Then they boarded a dining capsule and left the hotel to tour the forests and lakes while they ate. Lunch glided from its container and rolled towards them as they lounged in pneumochairs before a wraparound window. Crisp salad, grilled native fish, imported vegetables; a grated Centaurine cheese to sprinkle; flasks of cold rice beer; a rich, thick, spicy green liqueur afterwards. Completely passive, sealed in their moving capsule, they accepted food and drink and scenery, breathed the sparkling air pumped in from outside, watched gaudy birds flutter past them and lose themselves in the soft, drooping needles of the thickly-packed conifers of the woods. Boardman had carefully staged all this to create a mood, but his efforts were wasted, Muller knew. He could not be lulled this easily. He might take whatever job Boardman offered, but not because he had been fooled into false unwariness.

Marta was bored. She showed it by the detached response she gave to Boardman's inquiring lustful glances. The shimmering daywrap she wore was designed to reveal; as its long-chained molecules slid kaleidoscopically through their path of patterns they yielded quick, frank glimpses of thighs and breasts, of belly and loins, of hips and buttocks. Boardman appreciated the display and seemed ready to capitalize on Marta's apparent availability, but she ignored his unvoiced overtures entirely. Muller was amused by that. Boardman was not.

After lunch the capsule halted by the side of a jewel-like lake, deep and clear. The wall opened, and Boardman said, "Perhaps the young lady would like to swim while we get the dull business talk out of the way?"

"A fine idea," Marta said in a flat voice.

Arising, she touched the disrobing snap at her shoulder and let her garment slither to her ankles. Boardman made a great show of catching it up and putting it on a storage rack. She smiled mechanically at him, turned, walked down to the edge of the lake, a nude tawny figure whose tapering back and gently rounded rump were dappled by the sunlight slipping through the trees. For a moment she paused, shin-deep in the water; then she sprang forward and sliced the breast of the lake with strong steady strokes.

Boardman said, "She's quite lovely, Dick. Who is she?"

"A girl. Rather young, I think."

"Younger than your usual sort, I'd say. Also somewhat spoiled. Known her long?"

"Since last year, Charles. Interested?"

"Naturally."

"I'll tell her that," Muller said. "Some other time."

Boardman gave him a Buddha-smile and gestured towards the liquor console. Muller shook his head. Marta was back-stroking in the lake, the rosy tips of her breasts just visible above the serene surface. The two men eyed one another. They appeared to be of the same age, mid-fifties; Boardman fleshy and greying and strong-looking, Muller lean and greying and strong-looking. Seated, they seemed of the same height, too. The appearances were deceptive: Boardman was a generation older, Muller half a foot taller. They had known each other for thirty years.

In a way, they were in the same line of work—both part of the corps of nonadministrative personnel that served to hold the structure of human society together across the sprawl of the galaxy. Neither held any official rank. They shared a readiness to serve, a desire to make their gifts useful to mankind; and Muller respected Boardman for the way he had used those gifts during a long and impressive career, though he could not say that he liked the older man. He knew that Boardman was shrewd, unscrupulous, and dedicated to human welfare—and the combination of dedication and unscrupulousness is always a dangerous one.

Boardman drew a vision cube from a pocket of his tunic and put it on the table before Muller. It rested there like a counter in some intricate game, six or seven centimetres along each face, soft yellow against the polished black marble face of the table. "Plug it in," Boardman invited, "the viewer's beside you."

47

Muller slipped the cube into the receptor slot. From the centre of the table there arose a larger cube, nearly a metre across. Images flowered on its faces. Muller saw a cloud-wrapped planet, soft grey in tone, it could have been Venus. The view deepened and streaks of dark red appeared in the grey. Not Venus, then. The recording eye pierced the cloud layer and revealed an unfamiliar, not very Earthlike planet. The soil looked moist and spongy, and rubbery trees that looked like giant toadstools thrust upward from it. It was hard to judge relative sizes, but they looked big. Their pale trunks were coarse with shredded fibres, and curved like bows between ground and crown. Saucerlike growths shielded the trees at their bases, ringing them for about a fifth of their height. Above were neither branches nor leaves, only wide flat caps whose undersurfaces were mottled by corrugated processes. As Muller watched, three alien figures came strolling through the sombre grove. They were elongated, almost spidery, with clusters of eight or ten jointed limbs depending from their narrow shoulders. Their heads were tapered and rimmed with eyes. Their nostrils were vertical slits flush against the skin. Their mouths opened at the sides. They walked upright on elegant legs that terminated in small globe-like pedestals instead of feet. Though they were nude except for probably ornamental strips of fabric tied between their first and second wrists, Muller was unable to detect signs either of reproductive apparatus or of mammalian functions. Their skins were unpigmented, sharing the prevailing greyness of this grey world and were coarse in texture, with a scaly overlay of small diamond-shaped ridges.

With wonderful grace the three figures approached three of the giant toadstools and scaled them until each stood atop the uppermost saucerlike projection of a tree. Out of the cluster of limbs came one arm that seemed specially adapted; unlike the others, which were equipped with five tendril-shaped fingers arranged in a circlet, this limb ended in a needle-sharp organ. It plunged easily and deeply into the soft rubbery trunk of the tree on which its owner stood. A long moment passed, as if the aliens were draining sap from the trees. Then they climbed down and resumed their stroll, outwardly unchanged.

One of them paused, bent, peered closely at the ground. It scooped up the eye that had been witnessing its activities. The image grew chaotic; Muller guessed that the eye was being passed from hand to hand. Suddenly there was darkness. The eye had been destroyed. The cube was played out.

After a moment of troubled silence Muller said, "They look very convincing."

"They ought to be. They're real."

"Was this taken by some sort of extragalactic probe?"

"No," Boardman said. "In our own galaxy."

"Beta Hydri IV, then?"

"Yes."

Muller repressed a shiver. "May I play it again, Charles?"

"Of course."

He activated the cube a second time. Again the eye made the descent through the cloud layer; again it observed the rubbery trees; again the trio of aliens appeared, took nourishment from the trees, noticed the eye, destroyed it. Muller studied the images with cold fascination. He had never looked upon living sapient beings of another creation before. No one had, so far as he knew, until now.

The images faded from the cube.

Boardman said, "That was taken less than a month ago. We parked a drone ship fifty thousand kilometres up and dropped roughly a thousand eyes on Beta Hydri IV. At least half of them went straight to the bottom of the ocean. Most landed in uninhabited or uninteresting places. This is the only one that actually showed us a clear view of the aliens."

"Why has it been decided to break our quarantine of this planet?"

Boardman slowly let out his breath. "We think it's time we got in touch with them, Dick. We've been sniffing around them for ten years and we haven't said hello yet. That isn't neighbourly. And since the Hydrans and ourselves are the only intelligent races in this whole damned galaxy—unless something's hiding somewhere unlikely—we've come to the belief that we ought to commence friendly relations."

"I don't find your coyness very appealing," Muller said bluntly. "A full-scale council decision was taken after close to a year of debate, and it was voted to leave the Hydrans alone for at least a century—unless they showed some sign of going into space. Who reversed that decision, and why, and when?"

Boardman smiled his crafty smile. But Muller knew that the only way to avoid being drawn into his web was to take a frontal approach. Slowly Boardman said, "I didn't mean to seem deceptive, Dick. The decision was reversed by a council session eight months ago, while you were out Rigel way."

"And the reason?"

"One of the extragalactic probes came back with convincing evidence that there's at least one highly intelligent and quite superior species in one of our neighbouring clusters."

"Where?"

"It doesn't matter, Dick. Pardon me, but I won't tell you at this time."

"All right."

"Let's just say that from what we know of them now, they're much more than we can handle. They've got a galactic drive, and we can reasonably expect them to come visiting us one of these centuries—and when they do, we'll have a problem. So it's been voted to open contact with Beta Hydri IV ahead of schedule, by way of insurance against that day."

"You mean", Muller said, "that we want to make sure we're on good terms with the other race of our own galaxy before the extragalactics show up?"

"Exactly."

"I'll take that drink now," said Muller.

Boardman gestured. Muller tapped out a potent combination on the console, downed it quickly, ordered another. Suddenly he had a great deal to digest. He looked away from Boardman, picking up the vision cube and fingering it as though it were a sacred relic.

For a couple of centuries man had explored the stars without finding a trace of a rival. There were plenty of planets, and many of them were potentially habitable, and a surprising number were Earthlike to four or five places. That much had been expected. The sky is full of main-sequence suns, with a good many of the F-type and G-type stars most likely to support life. The process of planetogenesis is nothing remarkable, and most of those suns had complements of five to a dozen worlds, some of which were of the right size and mass and density slots to permit the retention of atmosphere and the convenient evolution of life, and a number of those worlds were situated within the orbital zone where they were best able to avoid extremes of temperature. So life abounded and the galaxy was a zoologist's delight.

But in his helter-skelter expansion out of his own system man had found only the traces of former intelligent species. Beasts laired in the ruins of unimaginably ancient civilizations. The most spectacular ancient site was the maze of Lemnos; but other worlds too had their stumps of cities, their weathered foundations, their burial grounds and strewn potsherds. Space became an archaeologist's delight, too. The collectors of alien animals and the collectors of alien relics were kept busy. Whole new scientific specialities burst into being. Societies that had vanished before the Pyramids had been conceived now underwent reconstruction.

A curious blight of extinction had come upon all the galaxy's other intelligent races, though. Evidently they had flourished so long ago that not even their decadent children survived; they were one with Nineveh and Tyre, blotted out, cut off. Careful scrutiny showed that the youngest of the dozen or so known extrasolar intelligent cultures had perished eighty thousand years earlier.

The galaxy is wide; and man kept on looking, drawn to find his stellar companions by some perverse mixture of curiosity and dread. Though the warp drive provided speedy transport to all points within the universe, neither available personnel nor available ships could cope with the immensity of the surveying tasks. Several centuries after his intrusion into the galaxy, man was still making discoveries, some of them quite close to home. The star Beta Hydri had seven planets; and on the fourth was another sapient species.

There were no landings. The possibility of such a discovery had been examined well in advance, and plans had been drawn to avoid a blundering trespass of unpredictable consequences. The survey of Beta Hydri IV had been carried out from beyond its cloud layer. Cunning devices had measured the activity behind that tantalizing grey mask. Hydran energy production was known to a tolerance of a few million kilowatt hours; Hydran urban districts had been mapped, and their population density estimated; the level of Hydran industrial development had been calculated by a study of thermal radiations. There was an aggressive, growing, potent civilization down there, probably comparable in technical level to late twentieth-century Earth. There was only one significant difference : the Hydrans had not begun to enter space. That was the fault of the cloud layer. A race that never has seen the stars is not likely to show much desire to reach them.

Muller had been privy to the frantic conferences that followed the discovery of the Hydrans. He knew the reasons why they had been placed under quarantine, and he realized that only much more urgent reasons had resulted in the lifting of that quarantine. Unsure of its ability to handle a relationship with nonhuman beings, Earth had wisely chosen to keep away from the Hydrans for a while longer; but now all that was changed.

"What happens now?" Muller asked. "An expedition?"

"Yes."

"How soon?"

"Within the next year, I'd say."

Muller tensed. "Under whose leadership?"

"Perhaps yours, Dick."

"Why 'perhaps'?"

"You might not want it."

"When I was eighteen," Muller said, "I was with a girl out in the woods on Earth, in the California forest preserve, and we made love, and it wasn't exactly my first time but the first time it worked out in any kind of proper way, and afterwards we were lying on our backs looking up at the stars and I told her I was going to go out and walk around among them. And she said, Oh, Dick, how wonderful, but of course it wasn't anything special I was saying. Any kid that age says it when he looks up at the stars. And I told her that I was going to discover things out in space, that men were going to remember me the way they remember Columbus and Mageellan and the early astronauts and all. I said I was going to be right in the front of whatever was happening, that I was going to move through the stars like a god. I was very eloquent. I went on like that for about ten minutes, until we were both carried away by the wonder of it all, and I turned to her and she pulled me down on top of her and I turned my backside to the stars and worked hard to nail her to the Earth, and that was the night I grew my ambitions." He laughed. "There are things we can say at eighteen that we can't say again."

"There are things we can do at eighteen that we can't do again either," said Boardman. "Well, Dick? You're past fifty now, right? You've walked in the stars. Do you feel like a god?"

"Sometimes."

"Do you want to go to Beta Hydri IV?"

"You know I do."

"Alone?"

Muller felt the ground give way before him, and abruptly it seemed to him that he was taking his first spacewalk again, falling freely towards all the universe. "*Alone?*"

"We've programmed the whole thing and concluded that to send a bunch of men down there at this point would be a mistake. The Hydrans haven't responded very well to our eye probes. You saw that: they picked the eye up and smashed it. We can't begin to fathom their psychologies, because we've never been up against alien minds before. But we feel that the safest thing—both in terms of potential manpower loss and in terms of impact on their society—is to send a single ambassador down there to them—one man, coming in peace, a shrewd, strong man who had been tested under a variety of stress situations and who will develop ways of initiating contact. That man may find himself chopped to shreds thirty seconds after making contact. On the other hand, if he survives he'll have accomplished

53

something utterly unique in human history. It's your option."

It was irresistible. Mankind's ambassador to the Hydrans! To go alone, to walk alien soil and extend humanity's first greeting to cosmic neighbours—

It was his ticket to immortality. It would write his name forever on the stars.

"How do you figure the chance of survival?" Muller asked.

"The computation is one chance in sixty-five of coming out whole, Dick. Considering that it's not an Earth-type planet to any great degree, you'll need a life-support system. And you may get a chilly reception. One in sixty-five."

"Not too bad."

"I'd never accept such odds myself," Boardman said, grinning.

"No, but I might." He drained his glass. To carry it off meant imperishable fame. To fail, to be slain by the Hydrans, even that was not so dreadful. He had lived well. There were worse fates than to die bearing mankind's banner to a strange world. That throbbing pride of his, that hunger for glory, that childlike craving for renown that he had never outgrown, drove him to it. The odds were not too bad.

Marta reappeared. She was wet from her swim, her nude body glossy, her hair plastered to the slender column of her neck. Her breasts were heaving rapidly, little cones of flesh tipped by puckered pink nipples. She might have been a leggy fourteen-year-old, Muller thought, looking at her narrow hips, her lean thighs. Boardman tossed her a drier. She thumbed it and stepped into its yellow field, making one complete turn. She took her garment from the rack and covered herself unhurriedly. "That was great," she said. Her eyes met Muller's for the first time since her return. "Dick, what's the matter with you? You look wide open— stunned. Are you all right?"

"Fine."

"What happened?"

"Mr. Boardman's made a proposition."

"You can tell her about it, Dick. We don't plan to keep it a secret. There'll be a galaxy-wide announcement right away."

"There's going to be a landing on Beta Hydri IV," Muller

54

said in a thick voice. "One man. Me. How will it work, Charles? A ship in a parking orbit, and then I go down in a powered drop-capsule equipped for return?"

"Yes."

Marta said "It's insane, Dick. Don't do it. You'll regret it forever."

"It's a quick death if things don't work out, Marta. I've taken worse risks before."

"No. Look, sometimes I think I've got a little precog. I see things ahead, Dick." She laughed nervously, her pose of cool sophistication abruptly shattering. "If you go there, I don't think you'll die. But I don't exactly think you'll live, either. Say you won't go. Say it, Dick!"

"You never officially accepted the proposition," Boardman pointed out.

"I know," Muller said. He got to his feet, nearly reaching the low roof of the dining capsule, and walked towards Marta, and put his arms around her, remembering that other girl so long ago under the California sky, remembering the wild surge of power that had come upon him as he swung over from the blaze of the stars to the warm, yielding flesh and the parting thighs beneath him. He held Marta firmly. She looked at him in horror. He kissed the tip of her nose and the lobe of her left ear. She shrank away from him, stumbled, nearly plunged into Boardman's lap. Boardman caught her and held her. Muller said. "You know what the answer has to be."

That afternoon one of the robot probes reached Zone F. They still had a distance to go; but it would not be long, Muller knew, before they were at the heart of the maze.

CHAPTER FOUR

"THERE HE is," Rawlins said. "At last!"

Via the drone probe's eyes he stared at the man in the maze. Muller leaned casually against a wall, arms folded; a big weatherbeaten man with a harsh chin and a massive wedge-shaped nose. He did not seem at all alarmed by the presence of the drone.

Rawlins cut in the audio pickup and heard Muller say, "Hello, robot. Why are you bothering me?"

The probe, of course, did not reply. Neither did Rawlins, who could have piped a message through the drone. He stood by the data terminal, crouching a little for a better view. His weary eyes throbbed. It had taken them nine local-time days to get one of their probes all the way through the maze to the centre. The effort had cost them close to a hundred probes; each inward extension of the safe route by twenty metres or so had required the expenditure of one of the robots. Still, that wasn't so bad, considering that the number of wrong choices in the maze was close to infinite. Through luck, the inspired use of the ship's brain, and a sturdy battery of sensory devices, they had managed to avoid all the obvious traps and most of the cleverer ones. And now they were in the centre.

Rawlins felt exhausted. He had been up all night monitoring this critical phase, the penetration of Zone A. Hosteen had gone to sleep. So, finally, had Boardman. A few of the crewmen were still on duty here and aboard the ship, but Rawlins was the only member of the civilian complement still awake.

He wondered if the discovery of Muller had been supposed to take place during his stint. Probably not. Boardman wouldn't want to risk blowing things by letting a novice handle the big moment. Well, too bad. They had left him on duty, and he had moved his probe a few metres inward, and now he was looking right at Muller.

He searched for signs of the man's inner torment.

They weren't obvious. Muller had lived here alone for so many years—wouldn't that have done something to his soul? And that other thing, the prank the Hydrans had played on him—surely that too would have registered on his face. So far as Rawlins could tell, it hadn't.

Oh, he looked sad around the eyes, and his lips were compressed in a taut, tense line. But Rawlins had been expecting something more dramatic, something romantic, some mirror of agony on that face. Instead he saw only the craggy, indifferent, almost insensitive-looking features of a tough, durable man in late middle age. Muller had gone grey, and his clothing was a little ragged; he looked worn and frayed himself. But that was only to be expected of a man who had been living this kind of exile for nine years. Rawlins wanted something more, something picturesque, a gaunt, bitter face, eyes dark with misery.

"What do you want?" Muller asked the probe. "Who sent you? Why don't you go away?"

Rawlins did not dare to answer. He had no idea of the gambit Boardman had in mind at this point. Brusquely he keyed the probe to freeze and sped away towards the dome where Boardman slept.

Boardman was sleeping under a canopy of life-sustaining devices. He was, after all, at least eighty years old—though he certainly didn't look it—and one way to keep from looking it was to plug oneself into one's sustainers every night. Rawlins was a trifle embarrassed to intrude on the old man when he was enmeshed in his paraphernalia this way. Strapped to Boardman's forehead were a couple of meningeal electrodes that guaranteed a proper and healthy progression through the levels of sleep, thus washing the mind of the day's fatigue poisons. An ultrasonic drawcock filtered dregs and debris from Boardman's arteries. Hormone flow was regulated by the ornate webwork hovering above his chest. The whole business was linked to and directed by the ship's brain. Within the elaborate life system Boardman looked unreal and waxy. His breathing was slow and regular; his soft lips were slack; his cheeks seemed puffy and loose-fleshed. Boardman's eyeballs were moving rapidly beneath the lids; a sign of dreaming, of upper sleep. Could he be awakened safely now?

Rawlins feared to risk it. Not directly, anyway. He ducked out of the room and activated the terminal just outside. "Take a dream to Charles Boardman," Rawlins said. "Tell him we found Muller. Tell him he's got to wake up right away. Say, Charles, Charles, wake up, we need you. Got it?"

"Acknowledged," said the ship's brain.

The impulse leaped from dome to ship, was translated into response-directed form, and returned to the dome. Rawlins' message seeped into Boardman's mind through the electrodes on his forehead. Feeling pleased with himself, Rawlins entered the old man's sleeproom once again and waited.

Boardman stirred. His hands formed claws and scraped gently at the machinery in whose embrace he lay.

"Muller—" he muttered.

His eyes opened. For a moment he did not see. But the waking process had begun, and the life system jolted his metabolism sufficiently to get him functioning again. "Ned?" he said hoarsely. "What are you doing here? I dreamed that—"

"It wasn't a dream, Charles. I programmed it for you. We got through to Zone A. We found Muller."

Boardman undid the life system and sat up instantly, alert, aware. "What time is it?"

"Dawn's just breaking."

"And how long ago did you find him?"

"Perhaps fifteen minutes. I froze the probe, and came right to you. But I didn't want to rush you awake, so—"

"All right. All right." Boardman had swung out of bed, now. He staggered a little as he got to his feet. He wasn't yet at his daytime vigour, Rawlins realized; his real age was showing. He found an excuse to look away, studying the life system to avoid having to see the meaty folds of Boardman's body.

When I'm his age, Rawlins thought, I'll make sure I get regular shape-ups. It isn't a matter of vanity, really. It's just

58

courtesy to other people. We don't have to look old if we don't want to look old. Why offend?

"Let's go," Boardman said. "Unfreeze that probe. I want to see him right away."

Using the terminal in the hall, Rawlins brought the probe back to life. The screen showed them Zone A of the maze, cosier-looking than the outer reaches. Muller was not in view. "Turn the audio on one way," Boardman said.

"It is."

"Where'd he go?"

"Must have walked out of sight range," Rawlins said. He moved the probe in a standing circle, taking in a broad sweep of low cubical houses, high rising archways, and tiered walls. A small cat-like animal scampered by, but there was no sign of Muller.

"He was right over there," Rawlins insisted unhappily. "He—"

"All right. He didn't have to stay in one place while you were waking me up. Walk the probe around."

Rawlins activated the drone and started it in a slow cruising exploration of the street. Instinctively he was cautious, expecting to find more traps at any moment, though he told himself a couple of times that the builders of the maze would surely not have loaded their own inner quarters with perils. Muller abruptly stepped out of a windowless building and planted himself in front of the probe.

"Again," he said. "Back to life, are you? Why don't you speak up? What's your ship? Who sent you?"

"Should we answer?" Rawlins asked.

"No."

Boardman's face was pressed almost against the screen. He pushed Rawlins' hands from the controls and went to work on the fine tuning until Muller was sharply in focus. Boardman kept the probe moving, sliding around in front of Muller, as though trying to hold the man's attention and prevent him from wandering off again.

In a low voice Boardman said, "That's frightening. The look on his face—"

"I thought he looked pretty calm."

"What do you know? I *remember* that man. Ned, that's a face out of hell. His cheekbones are twice as sharp as they used to be. His eyes are awful. You see the way his mouth turns down—on the left side? He might even have had a light stroke. But he's lasted well enough, I suppose."

Baffled, Rawlins searched for the signs of Muller's passion. He had missed them before, and he missed them now. But of course he had no real recollection of the way Muller was supposed to look. And Boardman, naturally, would be far more expert than he at reading character.

"It won't be simple; getting him out of there," Boardman said. "He'll want to stay. But we need him, Ned. We need him."

Muller, keeping pace with the drone, said in a deep gruff voice, "You've got thirty seconds to state your purpose here. Then you'd better turn around and get going back the way you came."

"Won't you talk to him?" Rawlins asked. "He'll wreck the probe!"

"Let him," said Boardman. "The first person who talks to him is going to be flesh and blood, and he's going to be standing face to face with him. That's the only way it can be. This has to be a courtship, Ned. We can't do it through the speakers of a probe."

"Ten seconds," said Muller.

He reached into his pocket and came out with a glossy black metal globe the size of an apple, with a small square window on one side. Rawlins had never seen anything like it before. Perhaps it was some alien weapon Muller had found in this city, he decided, for swiftly Muller raised the globe and aimed the window at the face of the drone probe.

The screen went dark.

"Looks like we've lost another probe," Rawlins said.

Boardman nodded. "Yes. The last probe we're going to lose. Now we start losing men."

2

The time had come to risk human lives in the maze. It was

60

inevitable, and Boardman regretted it, the way he regretted paying taxes or growing old or voiding waste matter or feeling the pull of strong gravity. Taxes, ageing, excretion, and gravity were all permanent aspects of the human condition, though, however much all four had been alleviated by modern scientific progress. So was the risk of death. They had made good use of the drone probes here, and had probably saved a dozen lives that way; but now lives were almost surely going to be lost anyhow. Boardman grieved over that, but not for long and not very deeply. He had been asking men to risk their lives for decades, and many of them had died. He was ready to risk his own, at the right time and in the right cause.

The maze now was thoroughly mapped. The ship's brain held a detailed picture of the inward route, with all the known pitfalls charted, and Boardman was confident that he could send drones in with a ninety-five per cent probability of getting them to Zone A unharmed. Whether a man could cover that same route with equal safety was what remained to be seen. Even with the computer whispering hints to him every step of the way, a man filtering information through a fallible, fatigue-prone human brain might not quite see things the same way as a lathe-turned probe, and perhaps would make compensations of his own in the course that would prove fatal. So the data they had gathered had to be tested carefully before he or Ned Rawlins ventured inside.

There were volunteers to take care of that.

They knew they were likely to die. No one had tried to pretend otherwise to them, and they would have it no other way. It had been put to them that it was important for humanity to bring Richard Muller voluntarily out of that maze, and that it could best be accomplished by having specific human beings—Charles Boardman and Ned Rawlins—speak to Muller in person, and that since Boardman and Rawlins were nonreplaceable units it was necessary for others to explore the route ahead of them. Very well. The explorers were ready, knowing that they were expendable. They also knew that it might even be helpful for the first few of them to die. Each death brought new information; successful traversals of the inward route brought none, at this point.

They drew lots for the job.

The man chosen to go first was a lieutenant named Burke, who looked fairly young and probably was, since military men rarely went in for shape-ups until they were in the top echelons. He was a short, sturdy, dark-haired man who acted as if he could be replaced from a template aboard the ship, which was not the case.

"When I find Muller," Burke said—he did not say *if*—"I tell him I'm an archaeologist. Right? And that if he doesn't mind, I'd like some of my friends to come inside also?"

"Yes," said Boardman. "And remember, the less you say to him in the way of professional-sounding noises, the less suspicious he's going to be."

Burke was not going to live long enough to say anything to Richard Muller, and all of them knew it. But he waved goodbye jauntily, somewhat stagily, and strode into the maze. Through a backpack he was connected with the ship's brain. The computer would relay his marching orders to him, and would show the watchers in the camp exactly what was happening to him.

He moved smartly and smoothly past the terrors of Zone H. He lacked the array of detection devices that had helped the probes find the pivot-mounted slabs and the deathpits beneath, the hidden energy flares, the clashing teeth set in doorways, and all the other nightmares; but he had something much more useful riding with him: the accumulated knowledge of those nightmares, gathered through the expenditure of a lot of probes that had failed to notice them. Boardman, watching his screen, saw the by now familiar pillars and spokes and escarpments, the airy bridges, the heaps of bones, the occasional debris of a drone probe. Silently he urged Burke on, knowing that in not too many days he would have to travel this route himself. Boardman wondered how much Burke's life meant to Burke.

Burke took nearly forty minutes to pass from Zone H to Zone G. He showed no sign of elation as he negotiated the passageway; G, they all knew, was nearly as tough as H. But so far the guidance system was working well. Burke was executing a sort of grim ballet, dancing around the obstacles, counting his steps, now leaping, now turning sideways, now straining to step over some treacherous strip of pavement. He was progressing nicely. But the computer was unable to warn him about the small toothy creature awaiting atop a gilded ledge forty metres inside Zone G. It was no part of the maze's design.

It was a random menace, transacting business on its own account. Burke carried only a record of past experiences in this realm.

The animal was no bigger than a very large cat, but its fangs were long and its claws were quick. The eye in Burke's backpack saw it as it leaped—but by then it was too late. Burke, half-warned, half-turned and reached for his weapon with the beast already on his shoulders and scrambling for his throat.

The jaws opened astonishingly wide. The computer's eye relayed an anatomical touch Boardman could well have done without: within the outer row of needle-sharp teeth was an inner one, and a third one inside that, perhaps for better chewing of the prey or perhaps just a couple of sets of replacements in case outer teeth were broken off. The effect was one of a forest of jagged fangs. A moment later the jaws closed.

Burke tumbled to the ground, clutching at his attacker. A trickle of blood spurted. Man and beast rolled over twice, tripped some secret waiting relay, and were engulfed in a gust of oily smoke. When the air was clear again neither of them was in view.

Boardman said a little later, "There's something to keep in mind. The animals wouldn't bother attacking a probe. We'll have to carry mass detectors and travel in teams."

That was how they worked it the next time. It was a stiff price to pay for the knowledge, but now they realized they had to deal with the wild beasts as well as with the cunning of ancient engineers. Two men named Marshall and Petrocelli, armed, went together into the maze, looking in all directions. No animal could come near them without telltaling its thermal output into the infrared pickups of the mass detectors they carried. They shot four animals, one of them immense, and had no trouble otherwise.

Deep within Zone G they came to the place where the distortion screen made a mockery of all information-gathering devices.

How did the screen work, Boardman wondered? He knew of Earth-made distorters that operated directly on the senses, taking perfectly proper sensory messages and scrambling them within the brain to destroy all one-to-one correlations. But this screen had to be different. It could not attack the nervous system of a drone probe, for the drones had no nervous systems in any meaningful sense of that term, and their eyes gave accurate reports of what they saw. Somehow what the drones had seen—and what they had reported to the computer—bore no relation to the real geometry of the maze at that point. Other drones, posted beyond the range of the screen, had given entirely different and much more reliable accounts of the terrain. So the thing must work on some direct optical principle, operating on the environment itself, rearranging it, blurring perspective, subtly shifting and concealing the outlines of things, transforming normal configurations into bafflement. Any sight organ within reach of the screen's effect would obtain a wholly convincing and perfectly incorrect image of the area, whether or not it had a mind to be tinkered with. That was quite interesting, Boardman thought. Perhaps later the mechanisms of this place could be studied and mastered. Later.

It was impossible for him to know what shape the maze had taken for Marshall and Petrocelli as they succumbed to the screen. Unlike the drone probes, which relayed exact accounts of everything that passed through their eyes, the two men were not directly hooked to the computer and could not transmit their visual images to the screen. The best they could do was describe what they saw. It did not match the images sent back by the probe eyes mounted on their back-packs, nor did it match the genuine configurations apparent from outside the screen's range.

They did as the computer said. They walked forward even where their own eyes told them that vast abysses lay in

64

their path. They crouched to wriggle through a tunnel whose roof was bright with the suspended blades of guillotines. The tunnel did not exist. "Any minute I expect one of those blades to fall and chop me in half," Petrocelli said. There were no blades. At the end of the tunnel they obediently moved to the left, towards a massive flail that lashed the ground in vicious swipes. There was no flail. Reluctantly they did not set foot on a plumply upholstered walkway that appeared to lead out of the region of the screen. The walkway was imaginary; they had no way of seeing the pit of acid that actually was there.

"It would be better if they simply closed their eyes," Boardman said. "The way the drones went through—minus all visuals."

"They claim it's too scary to do it like that," said Hosteen.

"Which is better—to have no visual information, or to have the wrong information?" Boardman asked. "They could follow the computer's orders just as well with their eyes closed. And there'd be no chance that—"

Petrocelli screamed. On the split screen Boardman saw the real configuration—a flat, innocuous strip of road—and the screen-distorted one relayed by the backpack eyes—a sudden geyser of flame erupting at their feet.

"Stand where you are!" Hosteen bellowed. "It isn't real!"

Petrocelli, one foot high in the air, brought it back into place with a wrenching effort. Marshall's reaction time was slower. He had been whirling to escape the eruption when Hosteen had called to him, and he turned to the left before he halted. He was a dozen centimetres too far out of the safe road. A coil of bright metal flicked out of a block of stone and wrapped itself about his ankles. It cut through the bone without difficulty. Marshall toppled and a flashing golden bar stapled him to a wall.

Without looking back, Petrocelli passed through the column of flame unharmed, stumbled forward ten paces, and came to a halt, safe beyond the effective range of the distortion screen. "Dave?" he said hoarsely. "Dave, are you all right?"

"He stepped off the path," said Boardman. "It was a quick

finish."

"What do you want me to do?"

"Stay put, Petrocelli. Get calm and don't try to go anywhere. I'm sending Chesterfield and Walker in after you. Wait right where you are."

Petrocelli was trembling. Boardman asked the ship's brain to give him a needle, and the backpack swiftly eased him with a soothing injection. Still rigid, unwilling to turn towards his impaled companion, Petrocelli stood quite still, awaiting the others.

It took Chesterfield and Walker close to an hour to reach the place of the distortion screen, and nearly fifteen minutes to shuffle through the few square metres the screen controlled. They did it with their eyes closed, and they didn't like that at all : but the phantoms of the maze could not frighten blind men, and in time Chesterfield and Walker were beyond their grasp. Petrocelli was much calmer by then. Warily, the three continued towards the heart of the maze.

Something would have to be done, Boardman thought, about recovering Marshall's body. Some other time, though.

3

The longest days of Ned Rawlins' life had been those spent on the journey to Rigel, four years before, to fetch his father's body. These days now were longer. To stand before a screen, to watch brave men die, to feel every nerve screaming for relief hour after hour after hour—

But they were winning the battle of the maze. Fourteen men had entered it so far. Four were dead. Walker and Petrocelli had made camp in Zone E; five more men had set up a relief base in F; three others were currently edging past the distortion screen in G and soon would join them. The worst was over for these. It was clear from the probe work that the curve of danger dropped off sharply past Zone F, and that there were practically no hazards at all in the three inner zones. With E and F virtually conquered, it should not be difficult to break through to those central zones where Muller, impassive and uncommunicating, lurked and waited.

Rawlins thought that he knew the maze completely by now. Vicariously he had entered it more than a hundred times; first through the eyes of the probes, then through the relays from the crewmen. At night in feverish dreams he saw its dark patterns, its curving walls and sinuous towers. Locked in his own skull he somehow made the circuit of that labyrinth, kissing death a thousand times. He and Boardman would be the beneficiaries of hard-won experience when their turns came to go inside.

Their turns were coming near.

On a chill morning under an iron sky he stood with Boardman just outside the maze, by the upsloping embankment of soil that rimmed the outer flange of the city. In the short weeks they had been here, the year had dimmed almost startlingly towards whatever winter this planet had. Sunlight lasted only six hours a day now, out of the twenty; two hours of pale twilight followed, and dawns were thin and prolonged. The whirling moons danced constantly in the sky, playing twisting games with shadows.

Rawlins, by this time, was almost eager to test the dangers of the maze. There was a hollowness in his gut, a yearning born of impatience and embarrassment. He had waited, peering into screens, while other men, some hardly older than himself, gambled their lives to get inside. It seemed to him that he had spent all his life waiting for the cue to take the centre of the stage.

On the screen, they watched Muller moving at the heart of the maze. The hovering probes kept constant checks on him, marking his peregrinations with a shifting line on the master chart. Muller had not left Zone A since the time he encountered the drone; but he changed positions daily in the labyrinth, migrating from house to house as though he feared to sleep in the same one twice. Boardman had taken care not to let him have any contact with them since the encounter with the drone. It often seemed to Rawlins that Boardman was stalking some rare and fragile beast.

Tapping the screen, Boardman said, "This afternoon we go inside, Ned. We'll spend the night in the main camp.

Tomorrow you move forward to join Walker and Petrocelli in E. The day after that you go on alone towards the middle and find Muller."

"Why are you going inside the maze, Charles?"

"To help you."

"You could keep in touch with me from out here," said Rawlins. "You don't need to risk yourself."

Boardman tugged thoughtfully at his dewlap. "What I'm doing is calculated for minimum risk this way."

"How?"

"If you get into problems," Boardman said, "I'll need to go to you and give you assistance. I'd rather wait in Zone F, if I'm needed, than have to come rushing in suddenly from the outside through the most dangerous part of the maze. You see what I'm telling you? I can get to you quickly from F without much danger. But not from here."

"What kind of problems?"

"Stubbornness from Muller. He's got no reason to co-operate with us, and he's not an easy man to deal with. I remember him in those months after he came back from Beta Hydri IV. We had no peace with him. He was never actually level-tempered before, but afterwards he was a volcano. Mind you, Ned, I don't judge him for it. He's got a right to be furious with the universe. But he's troublesome. He's a bird of ill omen. Just to go near him brings bad luck. You'll have your hands full."

"Why don't you come with me, then?"

"Impossible," Boardman said. "It would ruin everything if he even knew I was on this planet. I'm the man who sent him to the Hydrans, don't forget. I'm the one who in effect marooned him on Lemnos. I think he might kill me if he saw me again."

Rawlings recoiled from that idea. "No. He hasn't become that barbaric."

"You don't know him. What he was. What he's become."

"If he's as full of demons as you say, how am I ever going to win his trust?"

"Go to him. Look guileless and trustworthy. You don't have to practice that, Ned. You've got a naturally innocent

68

face. Tell him you're here on an archaeological mission. Don't let him know that we realized he was here all along. Say that the first you knew was when our probe stumbled into him—that you recognized him, from the days when he and your father were friends."

"I'm to mention my father, then?"

"By all means. Tell him who you are. It's the only way. Tell him that your father's dead, and that this is your first expedition to space. Work on his sympathies, Ned. Dig for the paternal in him."

Rawlins shook his head. "Don't get angry with me, Charles, but I've got to tell you that I don't like any of this. These lies."

"Lied?" Boardman's eyes blazed. "Lies to say that you're your father's son? That this is your first expedition?"

"That I'm an archaeologist?"

Boardman shrugged. "Would you rather tell him that you came here as part of a search mission looking for Richard Muller? Will that help win his trust? Think about our purpose, Ned."

"Yes. Ends and means. I know."

"Do you, really?"

"We're here to win Muller's co-operation because we think that he alone can save us from a terrible menace," Rawlins said stolidly, unfeelingly, flatly. "Therefore we must take any approach necessary to gain that co-operation."

"Yes. And I wish you wouldn't smirk when you say it."

"I'm sorry, Charles. But I feel so damned queasy about deceiving him."

"We need him."

"Yes. But a man who's suffered so much already—"

"We need him."

"All right, Charles."

"I need you, too," Boardman said. "If I could do this myself, I would. But if he saw me, he'd finish me. In his eyes I'm a monster. It's the same with anyone else connected with his past career. But you're different. He might be able to trust you. You're young, you look so damned virtuous, and you're the son of a good friend of his. You can get through to him."

"And fill him up with lies so we can trick him."

Boardman closed his eyes. He seemed to be containing himself with an effort.

"Stop it, Ned."

"Go on. Tell me what I do after I've introduced myself."

"Build a friendship with him. Take your time about it. Make him come to depend on your visits."

"What if I can't stand being with him?"

"Conceal it. That's the hardest part, I know."

"The hardest part is the lying, Charles."

"Whatever you say. Anyhow, show that you can tolerate his company. Make the effort. Chat with him. Make it clear to him that you're stealing time from your scientific work— that the villainous bastards who are running your expedition don't want you to have anything to do with him, but that you're drawn to him by love and pity and won't let him interfere. Tell him all about yourself, your ambitions, your love life, your hobbies, whatever you want. Run off at the mouth. It'll reinforce the image of the naïve kid."

"Do I mention the galactics?" Rawlins asked.

"Not obtrusively. Work them in somewhere by way of bringing him up to date on current events. But don't tell him too much. Certainly don't tell him of the threat they pose. Or a word about the need we have for him, you understand. If he gets the idea that he's being used, we're finished."

"How will I get him to leave the maze, if I don't tell him why we want him?"

"Let that part pass for now," Boardman said. "I'll coach you in the next phase after you've succeeded in getting him to trust you."

"The translation", Rawlins said, "is that you're going to put such a whopper in my mouth that you don't even dare tell me now what it is for fear I'll throw up my hands and quit."

"Ned—"

"I'm sorry. But—look, Charles, why do we have to *trick* him out? Why can't we just say that humanity needs him, and force him to come out?"

"Do you think that's morally superior to tricking him

70

out?"

"It's cleaner, somehow. I hate all this dirty plotting and scheming. I'd much rather help knock him cold and haul him from the maze than have to go through what you've planned. I'd be willing to help take him by force—because we really do need him. We've got enough men to do it."

"We don't," Boardman said. "We can't force him out. That's the whole point. It's too risky. He might find some way to kill himself the moment we tried to grab him."

"A stungun," said Rawlins. "I could do it, even. Just get within range and gun him down, and then we carry him out of the maze, and when he wakes up we explain—"

Boardman vehemently shook his head. "He's had nine years to figure out that maze. We don't know what tricks he's learned or what defensive traps he's planted. While he's in there I don't dare to take any kind of offensive action against him. He's too valuable to risk. For all we know he's programmed the whole place to blow up if someone pulls a gun on him. He's got to come out of that labyrinth of his own free will, Ned, and that means we have to trick him with false promises. I know it stinks. The whole universe stinks, sometimes. Haven't you discovered that yet?"

"It doesn't *have* to stink!" Rawlins said sharply, his voice rising. "Is that the lesson you've learned in all those years? The universe doesn't stink. Man stinks! And he does it by voluntary choice because he'd rather stink than smell sweet! We don't *have* to lie. We don't *have* to cheat. We could opt for honour and decency and—" Rawlins stopped abruptly. In a different tone he said, "I sound young as hell to you, don't I, Charles?"

"You're entitled to make mistakes," Boardman said. "That's what being young is for."

"You genuinely believe and know that there's a cosmic malevolence in the workings of the universe?"

Boardman touched the tips of his thick, short fingers together. "I wouldn't put it that way. There's no personal power of darkness running things, any more than there's a personal power of good. The universe is a big impersonal machine. As it functions it tends to put stress on some of its

71

minor parts, and those parts wear out, and the universe doesn't give a damn about that, because it can generate replacements. There's nothing immoral about wearing out parts, but you have to admit that from the point of view of the part under stress it's a stinking deal. It happened that two small parts of the universe clashed when we dropped Dick Muller on to the planet of the Hydrans. We had to put him there because it's our nature to find out things, and they did what they did to him because the universe puts stress on its parts, and the result was that Dick Muller came away from Beta Hydri IV in bad shape. He was drawn into the machinery of the universe and got ground up. Now we're having a second clash of parts, equally inevitable, and we have to feed Muller through the machine a second time. He's likely to be chewed again—which stinks—and in order to push him into a position where that can happen, you and I have to stain our souls a little—which also stinks—and yet we have absolutely no choice in the matter. If we don't compromise ourselves and trick Dick Muller, we may be setting in motion a new spin of the machine that will destroy all of humanity—and that would stink even worse. I'm asking you to do an unpleasant thing for a decent motive. You don't want to do it, and I understand how you feel, but I'm trying to get you to see that your personal moral code isn't always the highest factor. In wartime, a soldier shoots to kill because the universe imposes that situation on him. It may be an unjust war, and that might be his brother in the ship he's aiming at, but the war is real and he has his role."

"Where's the room for free will in this mechanical universe of yours, Charles?"

"There isn't any. That's why I say the universe stinks."

"We have no freedom at all?"

"The freedom to wriggle a little on the hook."

"Have you felt this way all your life?"

"Most of it," Boardman said.

"When you were my age?"

"Even earlier."

Rawlins looked away. "I think you're all wrong, but I'm not going to waste breath trying to tell you so. I don't have the words. I don't have the arguments. And you wouldn't listen anyway."

"I'm afraid I wouldn't, Ned. But we can discuss this some other time. Say, twenty years from now. Is it a date?"

Trying to grin, Rawlins said, "Sure. If I haven't killed myself from guilt over this."

"You won't."

"How am I supposed to live with myself after I've pulled Dick Muller out of his shell?"

"Wait and see. You'll discover that you did the right thing, in context. Or the least wrong thing, anyhow. Believe me, Ned. Just now you may feel that your soul will forever be corroded by this job, but it won't happen that way."

"We'll see," said Rawlins quietly. Boardman seemed more slippery than ever when he was in this avuncular mood. To die in the maze, Rawlins thought, was the only way to avoid getting trapped in these moral ambiguities; and the moment he hatched the thought, he abolished it in horror. He stared at the screen. "Let's go inside," he said. "I'm tired of waiting."

CHAPTER FIVE

MULLER SAW them coming closer, and did not understand why he was so calm about it. He had destroyed that robot, yes, and after that they had stopped sending in robots. But his viewing tanks showed him the men camping in the outer levels. He could not see their faces clearly. He could not see what they were doing out there. He counted about a dozen of them, give or take two or three; some were settled in Zone E, and a somewhat larger group in F. Muller had seen a few of them die in the outer zones.

He had ways of attacking. He could, if he cared to, flood Zone E with backup from the aqueduct. He had done that once, by accident, and it had taken the city almost a full day to clean things up. He recalled how, during the flood, Zone E had been sealed off, bulkheaded to keep the water from spilling out. If the intruders did not drown in the first rush, they would certainly blunder in alarm into some of the traps. Muller could do other things, too, to keep them from getting to the inner city.

Yet he did nothing. He knew that at the height of his inaction was a hunger to break his years of isolation. Much as he hated them, much as he feared them, much as he dreaded the puncturing of his privacy, Muller allowed the men to work their way towards him. A meeting now was inevitable. They knew he was there. (Did they know who he was?) They would find him, to their sorrow and to his. He would learn whether in his long exile he had been purged of his affliction so that he was fit for human company again. But Muller already was sure of the answer to that.

He had spent part of a year among the Hydrans; and then, seeing that he was accomplishing nothing, he entered his powered drop-capsule, rode it into the heavens, and, repossessed his orbiting ship. If the Hydrans had a mythology, he would become part of it.

Within his ship Muller went through the operations that would return him to Earth. As he notified the ship's brain of his presence, he caught sight of himself in the burnished metal plate of the input bank and it frightened him, a little. The Hydrans did not use mirrors. Muller saw deep new lines etched on his face, which did not bother him, and he saw a strangeness in his eyes, which did. The muscles are tense, he told himself. He finished programming his return and then went to the medic chamber and ordered a forty-db drop in his neural level along with a hot bath and a thorough massage. When he came out, his eyes still looked strange; and he had sprouted a facial tic, besides. He got rid of the tic easily enough, but he could do nothing about his eyes.

The eyes have no expression, Muller told himself. It's the lids that do the work. My eyelids are strained from living in the breathing suit so long. I'll be all right. It was a rough few months, but now I'll be all right.

The ship gulped power from the nearest designated donor star. The ship's rotors whirled along the axes of warp, and Muller, along with his plastic and metal container, was hurled out of the universe on one of the shortcut routes. Even in warp, a certain amount of absolute time loss is experienced as the ship zips through the stitch in the continuum. Muller read, slept, listened to music, and played a woman cube when the need got great. He told himself that the stiffness was going out of his facial expression, but he might need a mild shape-up when he got to Earth. This jaunt had put a few years on him.

He had no work to do. The ship duly popped from warp within the prescribed limits, 100,000 kilometres out from Earth, and coloured lights flashed on his communications board as the nearest traffic station signalled for his bearings. Muller instructed the ship to deal with the traffic station.

"Match velocities with us, Mr. Muller, and we'll send a pilot aboard to get you to Earth," the traffic controller said.

Muller's ship took care of it. The coppery globe of the traffic station appeared in sight. It floated just ahead of Muller for a while, but gradually his ship drew abreast of it.

"We have a relay message for you from Earth," the controller said. "Charles Boardman calling."

"Go ahead," said Muller.

Boardman's face filled the screen. He looked pink and newly-buffed, quite healthy, well rested. He smiled and put his hand forward. "Dick," he said. "God, it's great to see you!"

Muller activated tactile and put his hand on Boardman's wrist through the screen. "Hello, Charles. One in sixty-five, eh? Well, I'm back."

"Should I tell Marta?"

"Marta," Muller said, thinking for a moment. Yes. The blue-haired wench with the swivel hips and the sharp heels. "Yes. Tell Marta. It would be nice if she met me when I landed. Woman cubes aren't all that thrilling."

Boardman gave him a you-said-a-mouthful-boy kind of laugh. Then he changed gears abruptly and said, "How did it go?"

"Poorly."

"You made contact, though?"

"I found the Hydrans, yes. They didn't kill me."

"Were they hostile?"

"They didn't kill me."

"Yes, but—"

"I'm alive, Charles." Muller felt the tic beginning again. "I didn't learn their language. I can't tell you if they approved of me. They seemed quite interested. They studied me closely for a long time. They didn't say a word."

"What are they, telepaths?"

"I can't tell you that, Charles."

Boardman was silent for a while. "What did they do to you, Dick?"

"Nothing."

"That isn't so."

"What you're seeing is travel fatigue," Muller said. "I'm in good shape, just a little stretched in the nerve. I want to breathe real air and drink some real beer and taste real meat, and I'd like to have some company in bed, and I'll be as good as ever. And then maybe I'll suggest some ways of contact with the Hydrans."

"How's the gain on your broadcast system, Dick?"

"Huh?"

"You're coming across too loud," said Boardman.

"Blame it on the relay station. Jesus, Charles. What does the gain on my system have to do with anything?"

"I'm not sure," Boardman said. "I'm just trying to find out why you're shouting at me."

"I'm not shouting." Muller shouted.

Soon after that they broke contact. Muller had word from the traffic station that they were ready to send a pilot aboard. He got the hatch ready, and let the man in. The pilot was a very blond young man with hawklike features and pale skin. As soon as he unhelmeted he said, "My name is Les Christiansen, Mr. Muller, and I want to tell you that it's an honour and a privilege for me to be the pilot for the first man to visit an alien race. I hope I'm not breaking security when I say that I'd love to know a little about it while we're descending. I mean, this is sort of a moment in history, me being the first to see you in person since you're back, and if it's not an intrusion I'd be grateful if you'd tell me just some of the—highlights—of your—of—"

"I guess I can tell you a little," Muller said affably. "First, did you see the cube of the Hydrans? I know it was supposed to be shown, and—"

"You mind if I sit down a second, Mr. Muller?"

"Go ahead. You saw them, then, the tall skinny things with all the arms—"

"I feel very woozy," said Christiansen. "I don't know what's happening." His face was crimson, suddenly, and beads of sweat glistened on his forehead. "I think I must be getting sick. I—you know, this shouldn't be happening—" The pilot crumbled into a webfoam cradle and huddled there, shivering, covering his head with his hands. Muller, his voice still rusty from the long silences of his mission, hesitated helplessly. Finally he reached down to take the man's elbow and guide him towards the medic chamber. Christiansen whirled away as if touched by fiery metal. The motion pulled him off balance and sent him into a heap on the cabin floor. He rose to his knees and wriggled until he was as far away from Muller as it was possible to get. In a strangled voice he said, "Where is it?"

"That door here."

Christiansen rushed for it, sealed himself in, and rattled the door to make sure of it. Muller, astonished, heard retching sounds, and then something that could have been a series of dry sobs. He was about to signal the traffic station that the pilot was sick, when the door opened a little and Christiansen said in a muffled voice, "Would you hand me my helmet, Mr. Muller?"

Muller gave it to him.

"I'm going to have to go back to my station, Mr. Muller."

"I'm sorry you reacted this way. Christ, I hope I'm not carrying some kind of contagion."

"I'm not sick. I just feel—lousy." Christiansen fastened the helmet in place. "I don't understand. But I want to curl up and cry. Please let me go, Mr. Muller. It—I—that is—it's terrible. That's what I feel!" He rushed into the void hatch. In bewilderment Muller watched him cross the void to the nearby traffic station.

He got on the radio. "You better not send another pilot over just yet," Muller told the controller. "Christiansen folded up with instant plague as soon as he took his helmet off. I may be carrying something. Let's check it out."

The controller, looking troubled, agreed. He asked Muller to go to his medic chamber, set up the diagnostat, and transmit its report. A little while later the solemn chocolate-hued face of the station's medical officer appeared on Muller's screen and said, "This is very odd, Mr. Muller."

"What is?"

"I've run your diagnostat transmission through our machine. No unusual symptoms. I've also put Christiansen through the works without learning anything. He feels fine now, he says. He told me that an acute depression hit him the moment he saw you, and it deepened in a hurry to a sort of metabolic paralysis. That is, he felt so gloomy that he could hardly function."

"Is he prone to these attacks?"

"Never," the medic replied. "I'd like to check this out myself. May I come over?"

The medic didn't curl up with the miseries as Christiansen had done. But he didn't stay long, either, and when he left his face was glossy with tears. He looked as baffled as Muller. When the new pilot appeared twenty minutes later, he kept his suit on as he programmed the ship for planetary descent. Sitting rigidly upright at his controls, his back turned to Muller, he said nothing, scarcely acknowledged Muller's presence. As required by law, he brought the ship down until its drive system was in the grip of a groundside landing regulator, and took his leave. Muller saw the man's face, tense, sweat-shiny, tight-lipped. The pilot nodded curtly, and went through the hatch. I must have a very bad smell, Muller thought, if he could smell it through his suit like that.

The landing was routine.

At the starport he cleared Immigration quickly. It took only half an hour for Earth to decide that he was acceptable; and Muller, who had passed through these computer banks hundreds of times before, figured that that was close to the record. He had feared that the giant starport diagnostat would detect whatever malady he carried that his own equipment and the traffic station medic had failed to find; but he passed through the bowels of the machine, letting it bounce sonics off his kidneys, and extract some molecules of his various bodily fluids, and at length he emerged without the ringing of bells and the flashing of warning lights. *Approved.* He spoke to the Customs machine. Where from, traveller? Where bound? *Approved.* His papers were in order. A slit in the wall widened into a doorway and he stepped through, to confront another human being for the first time since his landing.

Boardman had come to meet him. Marta was with him. A thick brown robe shot through with dull metal enfolded Boardman; he seemed weighted down with rings, and his brooding eyebrows were thick as dark tropical moss. Marta's hair was short and sea-green; she had silvered her eyes and gilded the slender column of her throat, so that she looked like some jewelled statuette of herself. Remembering her wet and naked from the crystalline lake, Muller disapproved of

79

these changes. He doubted that they had been made for his benefit. Boardman, he knew, liked his women ornate; it was probable that they had been bedding in his absence. Muller would have been surprised and even a little shaken if they had not.

Boardman's hand encircled Muller's wrist in a firm greeting that incredibly turned flabby within seconds. The hand slipped away even before Muller could return the embrace. "It's good to see you, Dick," Boardman said without conviction, stepping back a couple of paces. His cheeks seemed to sag as though under heavy gravitational stress. Marta slipped between them and pressed herself against him. Muller seized her, touching her shoulderblades and running his hands swiftly down to her lean buttocks. He did not kiss her. Her eyes were dazzling as he looked within them and felt himself lost in rebounding mirror images. Her nostrils flared. Through her thin flesh he felt muscles bridling. She was trying to get free of him. "Dick," she whispered. "I've prayed for you every night. You don't know how I've missed you." She struggled harder. He moved his hands to her haunches and pushed inward so fiercely that he could imagine her pelvic cage yielding and flexing. His legs were trembling, and he feared that if he let go of her she would fall. She turned her head to one side. He put his cheek against her delicate ear. "Dick," she murmured, "I feel so strange—so glad to see you that I'm all tangled up inside—let go, Dick, I feel queasy somehow—"

Yes. Yes. Of course. He released her.

Boardman, sweating, nervous, mopped at his face, jabbed himself with some soothing drug, fidgeted, paced. Muller had never seen him look this way before. "Suppose I let the two of you have some time together, eh?" Boardman suggested, his voice coming out half an octave too high. "The weather's been getting to me, Dick. I'll talk with you tomorrow. Your accommodations are all arranged." Boardman fled. Now Muller felt panic rising.

"Where do we go?" he asked.

"There's a transport pod outside. We have a room at the Starport Inn. Do you have luggage?"

"It's all aboard the ship," Muller answered. "It can wait."

Marta was chewing at the corner of her lower lip. He took her by the hand and they rode the slidewalk out of the terminal room to the transportation pods. Go on, he thought. Tell me that you don't feel well. Tell me that mysteriously you've come down with something in the last ten minutes.

"Why did you cut your hair?" he asked.

"It's a woman's right. Don't you like it this way?"

"Not as much." They entered the pod. "Longer, bluer, it was like the sea on a stormy day." The pod shot off on a bath of quicksilver. She kept far to her side, hunched against the hatch. "And the makeup, too. I'm sorry, Marta. I wish I could like it."

"I was prettying for your homecoming."

"Why are you doing that with your lip?"

"What am I doing?"

"Nothing," he said. "Here we are. The room is booked already?"

"In your name, yes."

They went in. He put his hand on the registration plate. It flashed green and they headed for the liftshaft. The inn began in the fifth sublevel of the starport and went down for fifty levels; their room was near the bottom. Choice location, he thought. The bridal suite, maybe. They stepped into a room with kaleidoscopic hangings and a wide bed with all accessories. The roomglow was tactfully dim. Muller thought of months of woman cubes and a savage throbbing rose in his groin. He knew he had no need to explain any of that to Marta. She moved past him, into the personal room, and was in there a long while. Muller undressed.

She came out nude. All the tricky makeup was gone, and her hair was blue again.

"Like the sea," she said. "I'm sorry I couldn't grow it back in there. The room wasn't programmed for it."

"It's much better now," he told her.

They were ten metres apart. She stood at an angle to him, and he studied the contours of her frail but tough form, the small upjutting breasts, the boyish buttocks, the elegant thighs.

"The Hydrans," he said, "have either five sexes or none, I'm not sure which. That's a measure of how well I got to know them while I was there. However they do it, I think people have more fun. Why are you standing over there, Marta?"

Silently she came towards him. He put one arm around her shoulders and cupped his other hand over one of her breasts. At other times when he did that he felt the nipple pebble-hard with desire against his hand. Not now. She quivered a little, like a shy mare wanting to bolt. He put his lips to her lips, and they were dry, taut, hostile. When he ran his hand along the fine line of her jaw she seemed to shudder. He drew her down and they sat side by side on the bed. Her hand reached for him, almost unwillingly.

He saw the pain in her eyes.

She rolled away from him, her head snapping back hard on to the pillow, and he watched her face writhe with some barely suppressed agony. Then she took his hands in hers and tugged him towards her. Her knees came up and her thighs opened.

"Take me, Dick," she said stagily. "Right now!"

"What's the hurry?"

She tried to force him on to her, into her. He wasn't having it that way. He pulled free of her and sat up. She was crimson to the shoulders, and tears glistened on her face. He knew as much of the truth now as he needed to know, but he had to ask.

"Tell me what's wrong, Marta."

"I don't know."

"You're acting like you're sick."

"I think I am."

"When did you start feeling ill?"

"I—oh, Dick, why all these questions? Please, love, come close."

"You don't want me to. Not really. You're being kind."

"I'm—trying to make you happy, Dick. It—it hurts so much—so—much."

"What does?"

She wouldn't answer. She gestured wantonly and tugged

at him again. He sprang from the bed.

"Dick, Dick, I warned you not to go! I said I had some precog. And that other things could happen to you there besides getting killed."

"Tell me what hurts you."

"I can't. I—don't know."

"That's a lie."

"When did it start?"

"This morning. When I got up."

"That's another lie. I have to have the truth!"

"Make love to me, Dick. I can't wait much longer. I—"

"You what?"

"Can't—stand—"

"Can't stand what?"

"Nothing. Nothing." She was off the bed too, rubbing against him, a cat in heat, shivering, muscles leaping in her face, eyes wild.

He caught her wrists and ground the bones together. "Tell me what it is you can't stand much longer, Marta."

She gasped. He squeezed harder. She swung back, head lolling, breasts thrust towards the ceiling. Her body was oiled now with sweat. Her nakedness maddened and inflamed him.

"Tell me," he said. "You can't stand—"

"—being near you," she said.

CHAPTER SIX

WITHIN THE maze the air was somehow warmer and sweeter. The walls must cut off the winds, Rawlins thought. He walked carefully, listening to the voice at his ear.

Turn left ... three paces ... put your right foot beside the black stripe on the pavement ... pivot ... turn left ... .. four paces ... ninety-degree turn to the right ... immediately make a ninety-degree turn to the right again.

It was like a children's street game—step on a crack, break your mother's back. The stakes were higher here, though. He moved cautiously, feeling death nipping at his heels. What sort of people would build a place like this? Ahead an energy flare spurted across the path. The computer called off the timing for him. *One, two, three, four, five, GO!* Rawlins went.

Safe.

On the far side he halted flatfooted, and looked back. Boardman was keeping pace with him, unslowed by age. Boardman waved and winked. He went through the patterns, too. *One, two, three, four, five, GO!* Boardman crossed the place of the energy flare.

"Should we stop here for a while?" Rawlins asked.

"Don't be patronizing to the old man, Ned. Keep moving. I'm not tired yet."

"We have a tough one up ahead."

"Let's take it, then."

Rawlins could not help looking at the bones. Dry skeletons ages old, and some bodies that were not old at all. Beings of many races had perished here.

What if I die in the next ten minutes?

Bright lights were flashing now, on and off many times a second. Boardman, five metres behind him, became an eerie figure moving in disconnected strides. Rawlins passed his own hand before his face to see the jerky movements. It was

84

as though every other fraction of a second had simply been punched out of his awareness.

The computer told him: *Walk ten paces and halt. One. Two. Three. Walk ten paces and halt. One. Two. Three. Walk ten paces and halt. One. Two. Three. Proceed quickly to end of ramp.*

Rawlins could not remember what would happen to him if he failed to keep to the proper timing. Here in Zone H the nightmares were so thick that he could not keep them straight in his mind. Was this the place where a ton of stone fell on the unwary? Where the walls came together? Where a cob-web-dainty bridge delivered victims to a lake of fire?

His estimated lifespan at this point was two hundred and five years. He wanted to have most of those years. I am too uncomplicated to die yet, Ned Rawlins thought.

He danced to the computer's tune, past the lake of fire, past the clashing walls.

2

Something with long teeth perched on the lintel of the door ahead. Carefully Charles Boardman unslung the gun from his backpack and cut in the proximity-responsive target finder. He keyed it for thirty kilograms of mass and downward, at fifty metres. "I've got it," he told Rawlins, and fired.

The energy bolt splashed against the wall. Streaks of shimmering green sprouted along the rich purple. The beast leaped, limbs outstretched in a final agony, and fell. From somewhere came three small scavengers that began to rip it to pieces.

Boardman chuckled. It didn't take much skill to hunt with proximity-responsives, he had to admit. But it was a long time since he had hunted at all. When he was thirty, he had spent a long week in the Sahara Preserve as the youngest of a party of eight businessmen and government consultants on a hunt. He had done it for the political usefulness of making the trip. He had hated it all: the steaming air in his nostrils, the blaze of the sun, the tawny beasts dead against the sand, the boasting, the wanton slaughter. At thirty, one is not very tolerant of the mindless sports of the middle-aged. Yet he had stayed, because he thought it would be useful to him to become friendly with these men. It *had* been useful. He had never gone hunting again. But this was different, even with proximity-responsives. This was no sport.

3

Images played on a golden screen bracketed to a wall near the inner end of Zone H. Rawlins saw his father's face take form, coalesce with an underlying pattern of bars and crosses, burst into flame. The screen was externally primed; what it showed was in the eye of the beholder. The drones, passing this point, had seen only the blank screen. Rawlins watched the image of a girl appear. Maribeth Chambers, sixteen years old, sophomore in Our Lady of Mercies High School, Rockford, Illinois. Maribeth Chambers smiled shyly and began to remove her clothes. Her hair was silken and soft, a cloud of gold; her eyes were blue, her lips were full and moist. She unhinged her breast-binders and revealed two firm upthrust white globes tipped with dots of flame. They were high and close together, as though no gravity worked on them, and the valley between them was six inches deep and a sixteenth of an inch in breadth. Maribeth Chambers blushed and bared the lower half of her body. She wore small garnets set in the dimples just above her plump pink buttocks. A crucifix of ivory dangled from a golden chain around her hips. Rawlins tried not to look at the screen. The computer directed his feet; he shuffled along obediently.

"I am the Resurrection and the Life," said Maribeth Chambers in a husky, passionate voice.

She beckoned with the tips of three fingers. She gave him a bedroom wink. She crooned sweet obscenities.

Step around in aback here, big boy! Let me show you a good time. . . .

She giggled. She wriggled. She heaved her shoulders and made her breasts ring like tolling bells.

Her skin turned deep green. Her eyes slid about in her face. Her lower lip stretched forth like a shovel. Her thighs

86

began to melt. Patterns of flame danced on the screen. Rawlins heard deep throbbing ponderous chords from an invisible organ. He listened to the whispering of the brain that guided him and went past the screen unharmed.

4

The screen showed abstract patterns : a geometry of power, rigid marching lines and frozen figures. Charles Boardman paused to admire it for a moment. Then he moved on.

5

A forest of whirling knives near the inner border of Zone H.

6

The heat grew strangely intense. One had to tiptoe over the pavement. This was troublesome because none who had passed this way before had experienced it. Did the route vary? Could the city introduce variations? How hot would it get? Where would the zone of warmth end? Did cold lie beyond? Would they live to reach Zone E? Was Richard Muller doing this to prevent them from entering?

7

Maybe he recognizes Boardman and is trying to kill him. There is that possibility. Muller has every reason to hate Boardman, and he has had no chance to undergo social adjustment. Maybe I should move faster and open some space between Boardman and myself. It seems to be getting hotter. On the other hand, he would accuse me of being cowardly. And disloyal.

Maribeth Chambers would never have done those things. Do nuns still shave their heads?

8

Boardman found the distortion screen deep inside Zone G

perhaps the worst of all. He was not afraid of the dangers; Marshall was the only man who had failed to get past the screen safely. He was afraid of entering a place where the evidence of his senses did not correspond to the real universe. Boardman depended on his senses. He was wearing his third set of retinas. You can make no meaningful evaluations of the universe without the confidence that you are seeing it clearly.

Now he was within the field of the distortion screen.

Parallel lines met here. The triangular figures emblazoned on the moist, quivering walls were constructed entirely of obtuse angles. A river ran sideways through the valley. The stars were quite close, and the moons orbited one another.

What we now must do is close our eyes and not be deceived.

Left foot. Right foot. Left foot. Right foot. Move to the left slightly—slide your foot. More. More. A trifle more. Back towards the right. That's it. Start walking again.

Forbidden fruit tempted him. All his life he had tried hard to see clearly. The lure of distortions was irresistible. Boardman halted, planting each foot firmly. If you hope to get out of this, he told himself, you will keep your eyes closed. If you open your eyes you will be misled and go to your death. You have no right to die foolishly here after so many men have struggled so hard to teach you how to survive.

Boardman remained quite still. The silent voice of the computer, sounding a little waspish, tried to prod him on.

"Wait," said Boardman quietly. "I can look around a little if I don't move. That's the important thing, *not to move.* You can't get into trouble if you don't move."

The ship's brain reminded him of the geyser of flame that had sent Marshall to his death.

Boardman opened his eyes.

He was careful not to move. All about him he saw the negation of geometry. This was the inside of the Klein bottle, looking out. Disgust rose like a green column within him.

You are eighty years old and you know how the universe

88

should look. Close your eyes now, C.B. Close your eyes and move along. You're taking undue risks.

First he sought Ned Rawlins. The boy was twenty metres ahead of him, shuffling slowly past the screen. Eyes closed? Of course. All of them. Ned was an obedient boy. Or a frightened one. He wants to live through this, and he'd rather not see how the universe looks through a distortion screen. I'd like to have had a son like that. But I'd have changed him by this time.

Boardman began to lift his right leg, checked himself, reimplanted it on the pavement. Just ahead, pulsations of golden light leaped in the air, taking now the form of a swan, now the form of a tree. Ned Rawlins' left shoulder rose too high. His back was humped. One leg moved forward and the other moved backwards. Through golden mists Boardman saw the corpse of Marshall stapled to the wall. Marshall's eyes were wide open. Were there no bacteria of decay on Lemnos? Looking into those eyes Boardman saw his own curving reflection, all nose, no mouth. He closed his eyes.

The computer, relieved, directed him onward.

9

A sea of blood. A cup of lymph.

10

To die, not having loved—

11

This is the gateway to Zone F. I am now leaving death's other kingdom. Where is my passport? Do I need a visa? I have nothing to declare. Nothing. Nothing. Nothing.

3

A chill wind blowing out of tomorrow.

7

The boys camped in F were supposed to come out and meet us and lead us through. I hope they don't bother. We can make it without them. We just have to get past the screen, and we're all right.

5

I've dreamed this route so often. And now I hate it, even though it's beautiful. You have to admit that : it's beautiful. And probably it looks most beautiful just before it kills you.

3

Maribeth's thighs have small puckers in the flesh. She will be fat before she's thirty.

10

You do all sorts of things in a career. I could have stopped long ago. I have never read Rousseau. I have not had time for Donne. I know nothing of Kant. If I live I will read them now. I make this vow, being of sound mind and body and eighty years of age, I Ned Rawlins will I Richard Muller will read I will I I I will read I Charles Boardman.

13

14

On the far side of the gateway Rawlins stopped short and asked the computer if it was safe for him to squat down and rest. The brain said that it was. Gingerly, Rawlins lowered himself, rocked on his heels a moment, touched his knee to the cool pebble-textured pavement. He looked back. Behind him, colossal blocks of stone, set without mortar and fitted to a perfect truing, were piled fifty metres high, flanking a tall narrow aperture through which the solid form of Charles Boardman now was passing. Boardman looked sweaty and flustered. Rawlins found that fascinating. He had never seen the old man's smugness pierced before. But they had never come through this maze before, either.

Rawlins himself was none too steady. Metabolic poisons boiled in the tubes and channels of his body. He was drenched with perspiration so thoroughly that his clothing was working overtime to get rid of it, distilling the moisture and volatizing the substratum of chemical compounds. It was too early to rejoice. Brewster had died here in Zone F, thinking that his troubles were over once he got past the dangers of G. Well, they were.

"Resting?" Boardman asked. His voice came out thin and unfocused.

"Why not? I've been working hard, Charles." Rawlins grinned unconvincingly. "So have you. The computer says it's safe to stay here a while. I'll make room."

Boardman came alongside and squatted. Rawlins had to steady him as he balanced before kneeling.

Rawlins said, "Muller came this way alone and made it."

"Muller was always an extraordinary man."

"How do you think he did it?"

"Why don't you ask him?"

"I mean to," Rawlins said. "Perhaps by this time tomorrow I'll be talking to him."

"Perhaps. We should go on now."

"If you say so."

"They'll be coming out to meet us soon. They should have fixes on us by now. We must be showing up on their mass detectors. Up, Ned. Up."

They stood. Once again Rawlins led the way.

In Zone F things were less cluttered but also less attractive. The prevailing mood of the architecture was taut, with a fussy line that generated a tension of mismatched objects. Though he knew that traps were fewer here, Rawlins still had the sensation that the ground was likely to open beneath him at any given moment. The air was cooler here. It had the same sharp taste as the air on the open plain. At each of the street intersections rose immense concrete tubs in which jagged, feathery plants were standing.

"Which is the worst part for you so far?" Rawlins asked.

"The distortion screen," said Boardman.

"That wasn't so bad—unless you feel peculiar about walking through stuff this dangerous with your eyes closed. You know, one of those little tigers could have jumped us then, and we wouldn't have known about it until we felt the teeth in us."

"I peeked," said Boardman.

"In the distortion zone?"

"Just for a moment. I couldn't resist it, Ned. I won't try to describe what I saw, but it was one of the strangest experiences of my life."

Rawlins smiled. He wanted to congratulate Boardman on having done something silly and dangerous and human, but he didn't dare. He said, "What did you do? Just stand still and peek and then move on? Did you have any close escapes?"

"Once. I forgot myself and started to take a step, but I didn't follow through. I kept my feet planted and looked around."

"Maybe I'll try that on the way out," Rawlins said. "Just one little look can't hurt."

"How do you know the screen's effective in the other direction?"

Rawlins frowned. "I never considered that. We haven't tried to go *outward* through the maze yet. Suppose it's altogether different coming out? We don't have charts for that direction. What if we all get clipped coming out?"

"We'll use the probes again," said Boardman. "Don't worry about that. When we're ready to go out, we'll bring a bunch of drones to the camp in Zone F here and check this exit route the same way we checked the entry route."

After a while Rawlins said, "Why should there be any traps on the outward route, anyway? That means the builders of the maze were locking themselves in as well as locking enemies out. Why would they do that?"

"Who knows, Ned? They were aliens."

"Aliens. Yes."

15

Boardman remembered that the conversation was incomplete. He tried to be affable. They were comrades in the face of danger. He said, "And which has been the worst place for you so far?"

"That other screen farther back," Rawlins said. "The one that shows you all the nasty, crawling stuff inside your own mind."

"Which screen is that?"

"Towards the inside of Zone H. It was a golden screen, fastened to a high wall with metal strips. I looked at it and saw my father, for a couple of seconds. And then I saw a girl I once knew, a girl who became a nun. On the screen she was taking her clothes off. I guess that reveals something about my unconscious, eh? Like a pit of snakes. But whose isn't?"

"I didn't see any such things."

"You couldn't miss it. It was—oh, about fifty metres after the place where you shot the first animal. A little to your left, halfway up the wall, a rectangular screen—a trapezoidal screen, really, with bright white metal borders, and colours moving on it, shapes—"

"Yes. That one. Geometrical shapes."

"I saw Maribeth getting undressed," Rawlins said, sounding confused. "And you saw geometrical shapes?"

16

Zone F could be deadly too. A small pearly blister in the ground opened and a stream of gleaming pellets rolled out. They flowed towards Rawlins. They move with the malevolent determination of a stream of hungry soldier ants. They stung the flesh. He trampled a number of them, but in his annoyance and fervour he almost came too close to a suddenly flashing blue light. He kicked three pellets towards the light and they melted.

17

Boardman had already had much more than enough.

18

Their elapsed time out from the entrance to the maze was only one hour and forty-eight minutes, although it seemed much longer than that. The route through Zone F led into a pink-walled room where jets of steam blew up from concealed vents. At the far end of the room was an irising slot. If you did not step through it with perfect timing, you would be crushed. The slot gave access to a long low-vaulted passageway, oppressively warm and close, whose walls were blood-red in colour and pulsated sickeningly. Beyond the passageway was an open plaza in which six slabs of white metal stood on end like waiting swords. A fountain hurled water a hundred metres into the air. Flanking the plaza were three towers with many windows, all of different sizes. Prismatic spotlights played against the windows. No windows were broken. On the steps of one of the towers lay the articulated skeleton of a creature close to ten metres long. The bubble of what was undoubtedly a space helmet covered its skull.

19

Alton, Antonelli, Cameron, Greenfield, and Stein constituted the Zone F camp, the relief base for the forward group. Antonelli and Stein went back to the plaza in the middle of F and found Rawlins and Boardman there.

"It's just a short way on," Stein said. "Would you like to rest a few minutes, Mr. Boardman?"

Boardman glowered. They went on.

Antonelli said, "Davis, Ottavio, and Reynolds passed on to E this morning when Alton, Cameron, and Greenfield reached us. Petrocelli and Walker are reconnoitering along the inner edge of E and looking a little way into D. They say it looks a lot better in there."

"I'll flay them if they go in," Boardman said.

Antonelli smiled worriedly.

The relief base consisted of a pair of extrusion domes side by side in a little open spot at the edge of a garden. The site had been thoroughly researched and no surprises were expected. Rawlins entered one of the domes and took his shoes off. Cameron handed him a cleanser. Greenfield gave him a food pack. Rawlins felt ill at ease among these men. They had not had the opportunities in life that had been given him. They did not have proper education. They would not live as long, even if they avoided all of the dangers to which they were exposed. None of them had blond hair or blue eyes, and probably they could not afford to get shape-ups that would give them those qualifications. And yet they seemed happy. Perhaps it was because they never had to stop to confront the moral implications of luring Richard Muller out of the maze.

Boardman came into the dome. It amazed Rawlins how durable and tireless the old man was. Boardman said, laughing, "Tell Captain Hosteen he lost his bet. We made it."

"What bet?" asked Antonelli.

Greenfield said, "We think that Muller must be tracking us somehow. His movements have been very regular. He's occupying the back quadrant of Zone A, as far from the entrance as possible—if the entrance is the one he uses—and he swings around in a little arc balancing the advance party."

Boardman said, "Hosteen gave three to one we wouldn't get here. I heard him." To Cameron, who was a communications technician, Boardman said, "Do you think it's possible that Muller is using some kind of scanning system?"

"It's altogether likely."

"Good enough to see faces?"

"Maybe some of the time. We really can't be sure. He's had a lot of time to learn how to use this maze, sir."

"If he sees my face," said Boardman, "we might as well just go home without bothering. I never thought he might be scanning us. Who's got the thermoplastics? I need a new face fast."

20

He did not try to explain. But when he was finished he had a long sharp nose, lean, downcurving lips, and a witch's chin. It was not an attractive face. But it was not the face of Charles Boardman either.

21

After a night of unsound sleep Rawlins prepared himself to go on to the advance camp in Zone E. Boardman would not be going with him, but they would be in direct contact at all times now. Boardman would see what Rawlins saw, and hear what Rawlins heard. And in a tiny voice Boardman would be able to convey instructions to him.

The morning was dry and wintry. They tested the communications circuits. Rawlins stepped out of the dome and walked ten paces, standing alone looking inward and watching the orange glow of daylight on the pockmarked porcelain-like walls before him. The walls were deep black against the lustrous green of the sky.

Boardman said, "Lift your right hand if you hear me, Ned."

Rawlins lifted his right hand.

"Now speak to me."

"Where did you say Richard Muller was born?"

"On Earth. I hear you very well."

"Where on Earth?"

"The North American Directorate, somewhere."

"I'm from there," Rawlins said.

"Yes, I know. I think Muller is from the western part of the continent. I can't be sure. I've spent only a very little time on Earth, Ned, and I can't remember the geography. If it's important, I can have the ship look it up."

"Maybe later," said Rawlins. "Should I get started now?"

"Listen to me, first. We've been very busy getting ourselves inside this place, and I don't want you to forget that everything we've done up to this point has been a preliminary to our real purpose. We're here for Muller, remember."

"Would I forget?"

"We've been preoccupied with matters of personal survival. That can tend to blur your perspective : whether you yourself, individually, live or die. Now we take a larger view. What Richard Muller has, whether it's a gift or a curse, is of high potential value and it's your job to gain use of it, Ned. The fate of galaxies lies on what happens in the next few days between you and Muller. Aeons will be reshaped. Billions yet unborn will have their lives altered for good or ill by the events at hand."

"You sound absolutely serious, Charles."

"I absolutely am. Sometimes there comes a moment when all the booming foolish inflated words mean something, and this is one of those moments. You're standing at a crossroads in galactic history. And therefore, Ned, you're going to go in there and lie and cheat and perjure and connive, and I expect that your conscience is going to be very sore for a while, and you'll hate yourself extravagantly for it, and eventually you'll realize that you've done a deed of heroism. The test of your communications equipment is now ended. Get back inside here and let's ready you to march."

22

He went alone only a short distance this time. Stein and Alton accompanied him as far as the gateway to Zone E. There were no incidents. They pointed in the right direction, and he passed through a pinwheeling shower of corruscating azure sparks to enter the austere funereal zone beyond. As he negotiated the uphill ramp of the entrance, he caught sight of a socket mounted in an upright stone column. Within the darkness of the socket was something mobile and gleaming that could have been an eye.

"I think I've found part of Muller's scanning system," Rawlins reported. "There's a thing watching me in the wall."

"Cover it with your spray," Boardman suggested.

"I think he'd interpret that as a hostile act. Why would an archaeologist mutilate a feature like that?"

"Yes. A point. Proceed."

There was less of an air of menace about Zone E. It was

made up of dark, tightly-compacted low buildings which clung together like bothered turtles. Rawlins could see different topography ahead, high walls, and a shining tower. Each of the zones was so different from all the others that he began to think they had been built at different times : a core of residential sectors, and then a gradual accretion of trap-laden outer rings as the enemies grew more troublesome. It was the sort of thought an archaeologist might have; he filed it for use.

He walked a little way, and saw the shadowy figure of Walker coming towards him. Walker was lean, dour, cool. He claimed to have been married several times to the same wife. He was about forty, a career man.

"Glad you made it, Rawlins. Go easy there on your left. That wall is hinged."

"Everything all right here?"

"More or less. We lost Petrocelli about an hour ago." Rawlins stiffened. "This zone is supposed to be safe !"

"It isn't. It's riskier than F, and nearly as bad as G. We underestimated it when we were using the probes. There's no real reason why the zones *have* to get safer towards the middle, is there? This is one of the worst."

"To lull us," Rawlins suggested. "False security."

"You bet. Come on, now. Follow me and don't use your brain too much. There's no value in originality in here. You go the way the path goes, or you don't go anywhere."

Rawlins followed. He saw no apparent danger, but he jumped where Walker jumped, and detoured where Walker detoured. Not too far on lay the inner camp. He found Davis, Ottavio, and Reynolds there, and also the upper half of Petrocelli. "We're awaiting burial orders," said Ottavio. Below the waist there was nothing left. "Hosteen's going to tell us to bring him out, I bet."

"Cover him, at least," Rawlins told him.

"You going on into D today?" Walker asked.

"I may as well."

"We'll tell you what to avoid. It's new. That's where Petrocelli got it, right near the entrance to D, maybe five metres this side. You trip a field of some kind and it cuts you in half. The drones didn't trip it at all."

"Suppose it cuts everything in half that goes by?" Rawlins asked. "Except drones."

"It didn't cut Muller," Walker said. "It won't cut you if you step around it. We'll show you how."

"And beyond?"

"That's all up to you."

23

Boardman said, "If you're tired, stay here for the night."

"I'd rather go on."

"You'll be going alone, Ned. Why not be rested?"

"Ask the brain for a reading on me. See where my fatigue level is. I'm ready to go onwards."

Boardman checked. They were doing full telemetry on Rawlins; they knew his pulse rate, respiration count, hormone levels, and many more intimate things. The computer saw no reason why Rawlins could not continue without pausing.

"All right," said Boardman, "go on."

"I'm about to enter Zone D, Charles. This is where Petrocelli got it. I see the tripline—very subtle, very well hidden. Here I go past it. Yes. Ye-es. This is Zone D. I'm stopping and letting the brain get my bearings for me. Zone D looks a little cosier than E. The crossing shouldn't take long."

24

The auburn flames that guarded Zone C were frauds.

25

Rawlins said softly, "Tell the galaxies that their fate is in good hands. I should find Muller in fifteen minutes."

CHAPTER SEVEN

MULLER HAD often been alone for long periods. In drawing
up the contract for his first marriage he had insisted on a
withdrawal clause, the standard one; and Lorayn had not
objected, for she knew that his work might occasionally take
him to places where she would not or could not go. During
the eight years of that marriage he had enforced the clause
three times for a total of four years.

When they let the contract run out, Muller's absences were
not really a contributing factor. He had learned in those
years that he could stand solitude, and even that he thrived
on it in a strange way. We develop everything in solitude
except character, Stendhal had written; Muller was not sure
of that but, in any case, his character had been fully formed
before he began accepting assignments that took him unac-
companied to empty dangerous worlds. He had volunteered
for those assignments. In a different sense he had volunteered
to immure himself on Lemnos, and this exile was more painful to him that those other absences. Yet he got along. His
own adaptability astonished and frightened him. He had
not thought he could shed his social nature so easily. The
sexual part was difficult, but not as difficult as he had imagined it would be; and the rest—the stimulation of debate,
the change of surroundings, the interplay of personalities—
had somehow ceased quickly to matter. He had enough cubes
to keep him diverted, and enough challenges surviving in
this maze. And memories.

He could summon remembered scenes from a hundred
worlds. Man sprawled everywhere, planting the seed of
Earth on colonies of a thousand stars. Delta Pavonis VI, for
example : twenty light-years out, and rapidly going strange.
They called the planet Loki, which struck Muller as a whop-
ping misnomer, for Loki was agile, shrewd, slight of build,
and the settlers on Loki, fifty years isolated from Earth,

went in for a cult of artificial obesity through glucostatic regulation. Muller had visited them a decade before his illstarred Beta Hydri journey. It was essentially a troubleshooting mission to a planet that had lost touch with its mother world. He remembered a warm planet, habitable only in a narrow temperate belt. Passing through walls of green jungle bordering a black river; watching beasts with jewelled eyes jostling on the swampy banks; coming at last to the settlement, where sweaty Buddhas weighing a few hundred kilograms apiece sat in stately meditation before thatched huts. He had never seen so much flesh per cubic metre before. The Lokites meddled with their peripheral glucoreceptors to induce accumulation of body fat. It was a useless adaptation, unrelated to any problem of their environment; they simply liked to be huge. Muller recalled arms that looked like thighs, thighs that looked like pillars, bellies that curved and recurved in triumphant excess.

They had hospitably offered a woman to the spy from Earth. For Muller, it was a lesson in cultural relativity; for there were in the village two or three women who, although bulky enough, were scrawny by local standards and so approximated the norm of Muller's own background. The Lokites did not give him any of these women, these pitiful underdeveloped hundred-kilogram wrecks, for it would have been a breach of manners to let a guest have a subpar companion. Instead they treated him to a blonde colossus with breasts like cannonballs and buttocks that were continents of quivering meat.

It was, at any rate, unforgettable.

There were so many other worlds. He had been a tireless voyager. To such men as Boardmen he left the subtleties of political manipulation; Muller could be subtle enough, almost statesmanlike when he had to be, but he thought of himself more as an explorer than as a diplomat. He had shivered in methane lakes, had fried in post-Saharan deserts, had followed nomadic settlers across a purple plain in quest of their strayed arthropodic cattle. He had been shipwrecked by computer failure on airless worlds. He had seen the coppery cliffs of Damballa, ninety kilometres high. He had taken a swim in the gravity lake of Mordred. He had slept beside a multicoloured brook under a sky blazing with a trio of suns, and he had walked the crystal bridges of Procyon XIV. He had few regrets.

Now, huddled at the heart of his maze, he watched the screens and waited for the stranger to find him. A weapon, small and cool, nestled in his hand.

2

The afternoon unrolled swiftly. Rawlins began to think that he would have done better to listen to Boardman and spend a night in camp before going on to seek Muller. At least three hours of deepsleep to comb his mind of tension—a quick dip under the sleep wire, always useful. Well, he hadn't bothered. Now there was no opportunity. His sensors told him that Muller was just ahead.

Questions of morality and questions of ordinary courage suddenly troubled him.

He had never done anything significant before. He had studied, he had performed routine tasks in Boardman's office, he had now and then handled a slightly sensitive matter. But he had always believed that his real career still was yet to open; that all this was preliminary. That sense of a future beginning was still with him, but it was time to admit that he was on the spot. This was no training simulation. Here he stood, tall and blond and young and stubborn and ambitious, at the verge of an action which—and Charles Boardman had not been altogether hypocritical about that —might well influence the course of coming history.

Ping.

He looked about. The sensors had spoken. Out of the shadows ahead emerged the figure of a man. Muller.

They faced each other across a gap of twenty metres. Rawlins had remembered Muller as a giant and was surprised to see now that they were about the same height, both of them just over two metres high. Muller was dressed in a dark glossy wrap, and in this light at this hour his face was a study in conflicting planes and jutting prominences, all peaks and valleys.

In Muller's hand lay the apple-sized device with which he had destroyed the probe.

Boardman's voice buzzed in Rawlins' ear. "Get closer to him. Smile. Look shy and uncertain and friendly, and *very* concerned. And keep your hands where he can see them at all times."

Rawlins obeyed. He wondered when he would begin to feel the effects of being this close to Muller. He found it hard to take his eyes from the shiny globe that rested like a grenade in Muller's hand. When he was ten metres away he started to pick up the emanation from Muller. Yes. That must certainly be it. He decided that he would be able to tolerate it if he came no closer.

Muller said, "*What do you—*"

The words came out as a raucous shriek. Muller stopped, cheeks flaming, and seemed to be adjusting the gears of his larynx. Rawlins chewed the corner of his lip. He felt an uncontrollable twitching in one eyelid. Harsh breathing was coming over the audio line from Boardman.

Muller began again. "What do you want from me?" he said, this time in his true voice, deep, crackling with suppressed rage.

"Just to talk. Honestly. I don't want to cause any trouble for you, Mr. Muller."

"You know me!"

"Of course I do. Everyone knows Richard Muller. I mean, you were *the* galactic hero when I was going to school. We did reports on you. Essays about you. We—"

"Get out of here!" The shriek again.

"—and Stephen Rawlins was my father. I knew you, Mr. Muller."

The dark apple was rising. The small square window was facing him. Rawlins remembered how the relay from the drone probe had suddenly ceased.

"Stephen Rawlins?" The apple descended.

"My father." Rawlins' left leg seemed to be turning to water. Volatilized sweat drifted in a cloud about his shoulders. He was getting the outpouring from Muller more strongly now, as though it took a few minutes to tune to his wavelength. Now Rawlins felt the torrent of anguish, the sadness, the sense of yawning abysses sundering calm meadows. "I met you long ago," Rawlins said. "You had just come back from—let's see, it was 82 Eridani, I think, you were all tanned and windburned—I think I was eight years old, and you picked me up and threw me, only you weren't used to Earthnorm gravity and you threw me too hard, and I hit the ceiling and began to cry, and you gave me something to make me stop, a little bead that changed colours—"

Muller's hands were limp at his sides. The apple had disappeared into his garment.

He said tautly, "What was your name? Fred, Ted, Ed—that's it. Yes. Ed. Edward Rawlins."

"They started calling me Ned a little later on. So you remember me, then?"

"A little. I remember your father a lot better." Muller turned away and coughed. His hand slipped into his pocket. He raised his head and the descending sun glittered weirdly against his face, staining it deep orange. He made a quick edgy gesture with one finger. "Go away, Ned. Tell your friends that I don't want to be bothered. I'm a very sick man, and I want to be alone."

"Sick?"

"Sick with a mysterious inward rot of the soul. Look, Ned, you're a fine handsome boy, and I love your father dearly, if any of this is true, and I don't want you hanging around me. You'll regret it. I don't mean that as a threat, just a statement of fact. Go away. Far away."

"Stand your ground," Boardman told him. "Get closer. Right in, where it hurts."

Rawlins took a wary step, thinking of the globe in Muller's pocket and seeing from those eyes that the man was not necessarily rational. He diminished the distance between them by ten per cent. The impact of the emanation seemed to double.

He said, "Please don't chase me away, Mr. Muller. I just want to be friendly. My father would never have forgiven me if he could have found out that I met you here, like this, and didn't try to help you at all."

"*Would have? Could have found out?* What happened to your father?"

"Dead."

"When? Where?"

"Four years ago, Rigel XXII. He was helping to set up a tight-beam network connecting the Rigel worlds. There was an amplifier accident. The focus was inverted. He got the whole beam."

"Jesus. He was still young!"

"He would have been fifty in a month. We were going to come out and visit him and give him a surprise party. Instead I came out by myself to bring his body back."

Muller's face softened. Some of the torment ebbed from his eyes. His lips became more mobile. It was as though someone else's grief had momentarily taken him from his own.

"Get closer to him," Boardman ordered.

Another step; and then, since Muller did not seem to notice, another. Rawlins sensed heat : not real but psychical, a furnace-blast of directionless emotion. He shivered in awe. He had never really believed in any essential way that the story of what the Hydrans had done to Richard Muller was true. He was too sharply limited by his father's heritage of pragmatism. If you can't duplicate it in the laboratory, it isn't real. If you can't graph it, it isn't real. If there's no circuitry, it isn't real. How could a human being possibly be redesigned to broadcast his own emotions? No circuitry could handle such a function. But Rawlins felt the fringes of that broadcast.

Muller said, "What are you doing on Lemnos, boy?"

"I'm an archaeologist." The lie came awkwardly. "This is my first field trip. We're trying to carry out a thorough examination of the maze."

"The maze happens to be someone's home. You're intruding."

Rawlins faltered.

"Tell him you didn't know he was here," Boardman prompted.

"We didn't realize that anyone was here," said Rawlins.

"We had no way of knowing that—"

"You sent your damned robots in, didn't you? Once you found someone here—someone you knew damned well wouldn't want to have any company—"

"I don't understand," Rawlins said. "We had the impression you were wrecked here. We wanted to offer our help."

How easily I do this, he told himself!

Muller scowled. "You don't know why I'm here?"

"I'm afraid not."

"You wouldn't, I guess. You were too young. But the others—once they saw my face, they should have known. Why didn't they tell you? Your robot relayed my face, didn't it? You knew who it was in here. And they didn't tell you a thing?"

"I really don't understand—"

"Come close!" Muller bellowed.

Rawlins felt himself gliding forward, though he was unaware of taking individual steps. Abruptly he was face to face with Muller, conscious of the man's massive frame, his furrowed brow, his fixed, staring, angry eyes. Muller's immense hand pounced on Rawlins' wrist. Rawlins rocked, stunned by the impact, drenched with a despair so vast that it seemed to engulf whole universes. He tried not to stagger.

"Now get away from me!" Muller cried harshly. "Go on! Out of here! *Out!*"

Rawlins did not move.

Muller howled a curse and ran ponderously into a low glassy-walled building whose windows, opaque, were like blind eyes. The door closed, sealing without a perceptible opening. Rawlins sucked in breath and fought for his balance. His forehead throbbed as if something behind it were struggling to burst free.

"Stay where you are," said Boardman. "Let him get over his tantrum. Everything's going well."

3

Muller crouched behind the door. Sweat rolled down his sides. A chill swept him. He wrapped his arms about himself so tightly that his ribs complained.

He had not meant to handle the intruder that way at all.

A few words of conversation; a blunt request for privacy; then, if the man would not go away, the destructor globe. So Muller had planned. But he had hesitated. He had spoken too much and learned too much. Stephen Rawlins' son? A party of archaeologists out there? The boy had hardly seemed affected by the radiation except at very close range. Was it losing its power with the years?

Muller fought to collect himself and to analyse his hostility. Why so fearful? Why so eager to cling to solitude? He had nothing to fear from Earthmen; they, not he, were the sufferers in any contact he had with them. It was understandable that they would recoil from his presence. But there was no reason for him to withdraw like this except out of some paralysing diffidence, the encrusted inflexibilities of nine years of isolation. Had it come to that—a love of solitude for its own sake? Was he a hermit? His original pretence was that he had come here out of consideration for his fellow men, that he was unwilling to inflict the painful ugliness that was himself upon them. But the boy had wanted to be friendly and helpful. Why flee? Why react so churlishly?

Slowly Muller rose and undid the door. He stepped outside. Night had fallen with winter's swiftness; the sky was black, and the moons seared across it. The boy was still standing in the plaza, looking a little dazed. The biggest moon, Clotho, bathed him in golden light so that his curling hair seemed to sparkle with inner flame. His face was very pale, with sharply accentuated cheekbones. His blue eyes gleamed in shock, like those of one who has been slapped.

Muller advanced, uncertain of his tactics. He felt like some great half-rusted machine called into action after too many years of neglect. "Ned?" he said. "Look, Ned, I want to tell you that I'm sorry. You've got to understand, I'm not used to people. Not—used—to—*people*."

"It's all right, Mr. Muller. I realize it's been rough for you."

"Dick. Call me Dick." Muller raised both hands and spread them as if trying to cup moonbeams. He felt terribly cold. On the wall beyond the plaza small animal shapes leaped and danced. Muller said, "I've come to love my privacy. You can even cherish cancer if you get into the right frame of mind. Look, you ought to realize something. I came here deliberately. It wasn't any shipwreck. I picked out the one place in the universe where I was least likely to be disturbed, and hid myself inside it. But, of course, you had to come with your tricky robots and find the way in."

"If you don't want me here, I'll go," Rawlins said.

"Maybe that's best for both of us. No. Wait. Stay. Is it very bad, being this close to me?"

"It isn't exactly comfortable," said Rawlins. "But it isn't as bad as—as—well, I don't know. From this distance I just feel a little depressed."

"You know why?" Muller asked. "From the way you talk, I think you do, Ned. You're only pretending not to know what happened to me on Beta Hydri IV."

Rawlins coloured. "Well, I remember a little bit, I guess. They operated on your mind?"

"Yes, that's right. What you're feeling, Ned, that's me, my goddam soul leaking into the air. You're picking up the flow of neural current, straight from the top of my skull. Isn't it lovely? Try coming a little closer . . . that's it." Rawlins halted. "There," Muller said, "now it's stronger. You're getting a better dose. Now recall what it was like when you were standing right here. That wasn't so pleasant, was it? From ten metres away you can take it. From one metre away it's intolerable. Can you imagine holding a woman in your arms while you give off a mental stink like that? You can't make love from ten metres away. At least, *I* can't. Let's sit down, Ned. It's safe here. I've got detectors rigged in case any of the nastier animals come in, and there aren't any traps in this zone. Sit." He lowered himself to the smooth milky-white stone floor, the alien marble that made this plaza so sleek. Rawlins, after an instant of deliberation, slipped lithely into the lotus position a dozen metres away.

Muller said, "How old are you, Ned?"

"Twenty-three."

"Married?"

108

A shy grin. "Afraid not."

"Got a girl?"

"There was one, a liaison contract. We voided it when I took on this job."

"Ah. Any girls in this expedition?"

"Only woman cubes," said Rawlins.

"They aren't much good, are they, Ned?"

"Not really. We could have brought a few women along, but—"

"But what?"

"Too dangerous. The maze—"

"How many men have you lost so far?" Muller asked.

"Five, I think. I'd like to know the sort of people who'd build a thing like this. It must have taken five hundred years of planning to make it so devilish."

Muller said, "More. This was the grand creative triumph of their race, I believe. Their masterpiece, their monument. They must have been proud of this murderous place. It summed up the whole essence of their philosophy—kill the stranger."

"Are you just speculating, or have you found some clues to their cultural outlook?"

"The only clue I have to their cultural outlook is all around us. But I'm an expert on alien psychology, Ned. I know more about it than any other human being, because I'm the only one who ever said hello to an alien race. Kill the stranger : it's the law of the universe. And if you don't kill him, at least screw him up a little."

"We aren't like that," Rawlins said. "We don't show instinctive hostility to—"

"Crap."

"But—"

Muller said, "If an alien starship ever landed on one of our planets we'd quarantine it and imprison the crew and interrogate them to destruction. Whatever good manners we may have learned grow out of decadence and complacency. We pretend that we're too noble to hate strangers, but we have the politeness of weakness. Take the Hydrans. A substantial faction within our government was in favour of generating fusion in their cloud layer and giving their system an extra sun—*before* sending an emissary to scout them."

"No."

"They were overruled, and an emissary was sent, and the Hydrans wasted him. Me." An idea struck Muller suddenly. Appalled, he said, "What's happened between us and the Hydrans in the last nine years? Any contact? War?"

"Nothing," said Rawlins. "We've kept away."

"Are you telling me the truth, or did we wipe the bastards out? God knows I wouldn't mind that, but yet it wasn't their fault they did this to me. They were reacting in a standard xenophobic way. Ned, has there been a war with them?"

"No. I swear it."

Muller relaxed. After a moment he said, "All right. I won't ask you to fill me in on all the other news developments. I don't really give a damn. How long are you people staying on Lemnos?"

"We don't know yet. A few weeks, I suppose. We haven't even really begun to explore the maze. And then there's the area outside. We want to run correlations on the work of earlier archaeologists, and—"

"And you'll be here for a while. Are the others going to come into the centre of the maze?"

Rawlins moistened his lips. "They sent me ahead to establish a working relationship with you. We don't have any plan yet. It all depends on you. We don't want to impose on you. So if you don't want us to work here—"

"I don't," Muller told him crisply. "Tell that to your friends. In fifty or sixty years I'll be dead, and they can sniff around here then. But while I'm here I don't want them bothering me. Let them work in the outer four or five zones. If any of them sets foot in A, B, or C, I'll kill him. I can do that, Ned."

"What about me—am I welcome?"

"Occasionally. I can't predict my moods. If you want to talk to me, come around and see. And if I tell you to get the hell out, Ned, then get the hell out. Clear?"

Rawlins grinned sunnily. "Clear." He got to his feet. Muller, unwilling to have the boy standing over him, rose also. Rawlins took a few steps towards him.

Muller said, "Where are you going?"

"I hate having to talk at this distance, to shout like this. I can get a little closer to you, can't I?"

Instantly suspicious, Muller replied, "Are you some kind of masochist?"

"Sorry, no."

"Well, I'm no sadist either. I don't want you near me."

"It's really not that unpleasant—Dick."

"You're lying. You hate it like all the others. I'm like a leper, boy, and if you're queer for leprosy I feel sorry for you, but don't come any closer. It embarrasses me to see other people suffer on my account."

Rawlins stopped. "Whatever you say. Look, Dick, I don't want to cause troubles for you. I'm just trying to be friendly and helpful. If doing that in some way makes you uncomfortable—well, just say so, and I'll do something else. It doesn't do me any good to make things worse for you."

"That came out pretty muddled, boy. What is it you want from me, anyhow?"

"Nothing."

"Why not leave me alone?"

"You're a human being, and you've been alone here for a long time. It's my natural impulse to offer companionship. Does that sound too dumb?"

Muller shrugged. "I'm not much of a companion. Maybe you ought to take all your sweet Christian impulses and go away. There's no way you can help me, Ned. You can only hurt me by reminding me of all I can no longer have or know." Stiffening, Muller looked past the tall young man towards the shadowy figures cavorting along the walls. He was hungry, and this was the hour to begin hunting for his dinner. He said brusquely, "Son, I think my patience is running out again. Time for you to leave."

"All right. Can I come back tomorrow, though?"

"Maybe. Maybe."

The boy smiled ingenuously. "Thanks for letting me talk to you, Dick. I'll be back."

4

By troublesome moonlight Rawlins made his way out of Zone A. The voice of the ship's brain guided him back over the path he had taken inward, and now and then, in the safest spots, Boardman used the override. "You've made a good start," Boardman said. "It's a plus that he tolerated you at all. How do you feel?"

"Lousy, Charles."

"Because of the close contact with him?"

"Because I'm doing something filthy."

"Stop that, Ned. If I'm going to have to pump you full of moral reassurance every time you set out—"

"I'll do my job," said Rawlins, "but I don't have to like it." He edged over a spring-loaded stone block that was capable of hurling him from a precipice if he applied his weight the wrong way. A small toothy animal snickered at him as he crossed. On the far side, Rawlins prodded the wall in a yielding place and won admission to Zone B. He glanced at the lintel and saw the recessed slot of the visual pickup and smiled into it, just in case Muller was watching him withdraw.

He saw now why Muller had chosen to maroon himself here. Under similar circumstances he might have done the same thing. Or worse. Muller carried, thanks to the Hydrans, a deformity of the soul in an era when deformity was obsolete. It was an aesthetic crime to lack a limb or an eye or a nose; these things were easily repaired, and one owed it to one's fellow man to get a shape-up and obliterate troublesome imperfections. To inflict one's flaws on society was clearly an antisocial act.

But no shape-up surgeon could do a cosmetic job on what Muller had. The only cure was separation from society. A weaker man would have chosen death : Muller had picked exile.

Rawlins still throbbed with the impact of that brief moment of direct contact. For an instant he had received from Muller a formless incoherent emanation of raw emotion, the inner self-spilling out involuntarily and wordlessly. The flow of uncontrollable innerness was painful and depressing to receive.

It was not true telepathy that the Hydrans had given him. Muller could not "read" minds, nor could he communicate his thoughts to others. What came forth was this gush of self : a torrent of raw despair, a river of regrets and sorrows, all the sewage of a soul. He could not hold it back. For that eternal moment Rawlins had been bathed in it; the rest of the time he had merely picked up a vague and general sense of distress.

He could generate his own concretenesses out of that raw flow. Muller's sorrows were not unique to himself; what he offered was nothing more than an awareness of the punishments the universe devises for its inhabitants. At that moment Rawlins had felt that he was tuned to every discord in creation : the missed chances, the failed loves, the hasty words, the unfair griefs, the hungers, the greeds, the lusts, the knife of envy, the acid of frustration, the fang of time, the death of small insects in winter, the tears of things. He had known aging, loss, impotence, fury, helplessness, loneliness, desolation, self-contempt, and madness. It was a silent shriek of cosmic anger.

Are we all like that? He wondered. Is the same broadcast coming from me, and from Boardman, and from my mother, and from the girl I used to love? Do we walk about like beacons fixed to a frequency we can't receive? Thank God, then. That's a song too painful to hear.

Boardman said, "Wake up, Ned. Stop brooding and watch out for trouble. You're almost in Zone C now."

"'Charles, how did you feel the first time you came close to Muller?"

"We'll discuss that later."

"Did you feel as if you knew what human beings were all about for the first time?"

"I said we'll discuss—"

"Let me say what I want to say, Charles. I'm not in any danger here. I just looked into a man's soul, and I'm shaken by it. But—listen, Charles—he isn't really like that. He's a *good* man. That stuff he radiates, it's just noise. It's a kind of sludge that doesn't tell you a real thing about Dick Muller. It's noise we aren't meant to hear, and the signal's altogether different—like when you open an amplifier up to the stars, full blast, and you get that rasping of the spectrum, you know, and some of the most beautiful stars give you the most terrible noises, but that's just an amplifier response, it has nothing to do with the quality of the star itself, it—it—"

"*Ned.*"

"I'm sorry, Charles."

"Get back to camp. We all agree that Dick Muller's a fine human being. That's why we need him. We need you, too, so shut your mouth and watch your step. Easy, now. Calm. Calm. Calm. What's that animal on your left? Hurry along, Ned. But stay calm. That's the way, son. Calm."

CHAPTER EIGHT

When they met again the next morning it was easier for both of them. Rawlins, having slept well under the sleep wire, went to the heart of the maze and found Muller standing beside a tall flat-sided spike of dark metal at the edge of the great plaza.

"What do you make of this?" Muller asked conversationally as Rawlins approached. "There are eight of these, one at each corner. I've been watching them for years. They turn. Look here." Muller pointed to one face of the pylon. Rawlins came close, and when he was ten metres away he picked up Muller's emanation. Nevertheless, he forced himself to go closer. He had not been so close yesterday except in that one chilling moment when Muller had seized him and pulled him near.

"You see this?" Muller asked, tapping the spike.

"A mark."

"It took me close to six months to cut it. I used a sliver from the crystalline outcropping set in that wall yonder. Every day for an hour or two I'd scrape away, until there was a visible mark in the metal. I've been watching that mark. In the course of one local year it turns all the way around. So the spikes are moving. You can't see it, but they do. They're some kind of calendars."

"Do they—can you—have you ever—"

"You aren't making sense, boy."

"I'm sorry." Rawlins backed away, trying hard to hide the impact of Muller's nearness. He was flushed and shaken. At five metres the effect was not so agonizing, and he stayed there, making an effort, telling himself that he was developing a tolerance for it.

"You were saying?"

"Is this the only one you've been watching?"

"I've scratched a few of the others. I'm convinced that

they all turn. I haven't found the mechanism. Underneath this city, you know, there's some kind of fantastic brain. It's millions of years old, but it still works. Perhaps it's some sort of liquid metal with cognition elements floating in it. It turns these pylons and runs the water supply and cleans the streets."

"And operates the traps."

"And operates the traps," Muller said. "But I haven't been able to find a sign of it. I've done some digging here and there, but I find only dirt below. Maybe you archaeologist bastards will locate the city's brain. Eh? Any clues?"

"I don't think so," said Rawlins.

"You don't sound very definite."

"I'm not. I haven't taken part in any of the work within the city." Rawlins smiled shyly. The quick facial movement annoyed him and drew reproof from Boardman, who pointed out over the monitor circuit that the shy smile always announced an upcoming lie and that it wouldn't be long before Muller caught on. Rawlins said, "Most of the time I was outside the city, directing the entry operations. And then when I got in, I came right in here. So I don't know what the others may have discovered so far. If anything."

"Are they going to rip up the streets?" Muller asked.

"I don't think so. We don't dig so much any more. We use scanners and sensors and probe beams." Glibly, impressed with his own improvisations, he went on headlong. "Archaeology used to be destructive, of course. To find out what was under a pyramid we had to take the pyramid apart. But now we can do a lot with probes. That's the new school, you understand, looking into the ground without digging, and thus preserving the monuments of the past for—"

"On one of the planets of Epsilon Indi," said Muller, "a team of archaeologists completely dismantled an ancient alien burial pavilion about fifteen years ago, and then found it impossible to put the thing back together because they couldn't comprehend the structural integrity of the building. When they tried, it fell apart and was a total loss. I happened to see the ruins a few months later. You know the case, of course."

Rawlins didn't. He said, reddening, "Well, there are always bunglers in any discipline—"

"I hope there are none here. I don't want the maze damaged. Not that there's much chance of that. The maze defends itself quite well." Muller strolled casually away from the pylon. Rawlins eased as the distance between them grew, but Boardman warned him to follow. The tactics for damping Muller's mistrust included a deliberate and rigorous self-exposure to the emotion field. Muller was not looking back, and said, half to himself, "The cages are closed again."

"Cages?"

"Look down there—into that street branching out of the plaza."

Rawlins saw an alcove against a building wall. Rising from the ground were a dozen or more curving bars of white stone that disappeared into the wall at a height of about four metres, forming a kind of cage. He could see a second such cage farther down the street.

Muller said, "There are about twenty of them, arranged symmetrically in the streets off the plaza. Three times since I've been here the cages have opened. Those bars slide into the street, somehow, and disappear. The third time was two nights ago. I've never seen the cages either open or close, and I've missed it again."

"What do you think the cages were used for?" Rawlins asked.

"To hold dangerous beasts. Or captured enemies. What else would you use a cage for?"

"And when they open now—"

"They city's still trying to serve its people. There are enemies in the outer zones. The cages are ready in case any of the enemies are captured."

"You mean us?"

"Yes. Enemies." Muller's eyes glittered with sudden paranoid fury; it was alarming how easily he slipped from rational discourse to that cold blaze. "*Homo sapiens*. The most dangerous, the most ruthless, the most despicable beast in the universe!"

"You say it as if you believe it."

"I do."

"Come on," Rawlins said. "You devoted your life to serving mankind. You can't possibly believe—"

"I devoted my life," said Muller slowly, "to serving Richard Muller." He swung around so that he faced Rawlins squarely. They were only six or seven metres apart. The emanation seemed almost as strong as though they were nose to nose. Muller said, "I gave less of a damn for humanity than you might think, boy. I saw the stars, and I wanted them. I aspired after the condition of a deity. One world wasn't enough for me. I was hungry to have them all. So I built a career that would take me to the stars. I risked my life a thousand times. I endured fantastic extremes of temperature. I rotted my lungs with crazy gases, and had to be rebuilt from the inside out. I ate foods that would sicken you to hear about. Kids like you worshipped me and wrote essays about my selfless dedication to man, my tireless quest for knowledge. Let me get you straight on that. I'm about as selfless as Columbus and Magellan and Marco Polo. They were great explorers, yes, but they also looked for a fat profit. The profit I wanted was in here. I wanted to stand a hundred kilometres high. I wanted golden statues of me on a thousand worlds. You know poetry? Fame is the spur. That last infirmity of noble mind. Milton. Do you know your Greeks, too? When a man overreaches himself, the gods cast him down. It's called *hybris*. I had a bad case of it. When I dropped through the clouds to visit the Hydrans, I felt like a god. Christ, I *was* a god. And when I left, up through the clouds again. To the Hydrans I'm a god, all right. I thought it then : I'm in their myths, they'll always tell my story. The mutilated god. The martyred god. The being who came down among them and made them so uncomfortable that they had to fix him. But—"

"The cage—"

"Let me finish!" Muller rapped. "You see, the truth is, I wasn't a god, only a rotten mortal human being who had delusions of godhood, and the real gods saw to it that I learned my lesson. They decided to remind me of the hairy beast inside the plastic clothing. To call my attention to the animal brain under the lofty cranium. So they arranged it for the Hydrans to perform a clever little surgical trick on my brain, one of their specialities, I guess. I don't know if the Hydrans were being malicious for the hell of it or whether they were genuinely trying to cure me of a defect, my inability to let my emotions get out to them. Aliens. You figure them out. But they did their little job. And then I came back to Earth. Hero and leper all at once. Stand near me and you get sick. Why? It reminds you that *you're* an animal too, because you get a full dose of me. So we go round and round in our endless feedback. You hate me because you learn things about your own soul by getting near me. And I hate you because you must draw back from me. What I am, you see, is a plague carrier, and the plague I carry is the truth. My message is that it's a lucky thing for humanity that we're shut up each in his own skull. Because if we had even a little drop of telepathy, even the blurry nonverbal thing I've got, we'd be unable to stand each other. Human society would be impossible. The Hydrans can reach right into each other's mind, and they seem to like it. But we can't. And that's why I say that man must be the most despicable beast in the whole universe. He can't even take the reek of his own kind, soul to soul!"

Rawlins said, "The cage seems to be opening."

"What? Let me look!" Muller came jostling forward. Unable to step aside rapidly enough, Rawlins received the brunt of the emanation. It was not as painful this time. Images of autumn came to him: withered leaves, dying flowers, a dusty wind, early twilight. More regret than anguish over the shortness of life, the necessity of the condition. Meanwhile Muller, oblivious, was peering intently at the alabaster bars of the cage.

"It's withdrawn by several centimetres already. Why didn't you tell me?"

"I tried to. But you weren't listening."

"No. No. My damned soliloquizing." Muller chuckled. "Ned, I've been waiting years to see this. The cage actually in motion! Look how smoothly it moves, gliding into the ground. This is strange, Ned. It's never opened twice the same year before, and here it's opening for the second time this week."

"Maybe you've just failed to notice a lot of the other openings," Rawlins suggested. "While you slept, maybe—"

"I doubt it. Look at that!"

"Why do you think it's doing it right now?"

"Enemies all around," said Muller. "The city accepts me as a native by now. I've been here so long. But it must be trying to get you into a cage. The enemy. Man."

The cage was fully open now. There was no sign of the bars except the row of small openings in the pavement.

Rawlins said, "Have you ever tried to put anything in the cages? Animals?"

"Yes. I dragged a big dead beast inside one. Nothing happened. Then I caught some live little ones. Nothing happened." He frowned. "I once thought of stepping into the cage myself to see if it would close automatically when it sensed a live human being. But I didn't. When you're alone, you don't try experiments like that." He paused a moment, "How would *you* like to help me in a little experiment right now, eh, Ned?"

Rawlins caught his breath. The thin air abruptly seemed like fire in his lungs.

Muller said quietly, "Just step across into the alcove and wait a minute or so. See if the cage closes on you. That would be important to know."

"And if it does," Rawlins said, not taking him seriously, "do you have a key to let me out?"

"I have a few weapons. We can always blast you out by lasing the bars."

"That's destructive. You warned me not to destroy anything here."

"Sometimes you destroy in order to learn. Go on, Ned. Step into the alcove."

Muller's voice grew flat and strange. He was standing in an odd expectant half-crouch, hands at his sides, fingertips bent inward towards his thighs. As though he's going to throw me into the cage himself, Rawlins thought.

Boardman said quietly in Rawlins' ear, "Do as he says,

Ned. Get into the cage. Show him that you trust him."

I trust *him*, Rawlins told himself, but I don't trust that cage.

He had uncomfortable visions of the floor of the cage dropping out as soon as the bars were in place : of himself dumped into some underground vat of acid or lake of fire. The disposal pit for trapped enemies. What assurance do I have that it isn't like that?

"Do it, Ned," Boardman murmured.

It was a grand, crazy gesture. Rawlins stepped over the row of small openings and stood with his back to the wall. Almost at once the curving bars rose from the ground and locked themselves seamlessly into place above his head. The floor seemed stable. No death-rays lashed out at him. His worst fears were not realized; but he was a prisoner.

"Fascinating," Muller said. "It must scan for intelligence. When I tried with animals, nothing happened. Dead or alive. What do you make of that, Ned?"

"I'm very glad to have helped your research. I'd be happier if you'd let me out now."

"I can't control the movements of the bars."

"You said you'd lase them open."

"But why be destructive so fast? Let's wait, shall we? Perhaps the bars will open again of their own accord. You're perfectly safe in there. I'll bring you food, if you have to eat. Will your people miss you if you're not back by nightfall?"

"I'll send a message to them," said Rawlins glumly. "But I hope that I'm out by then."

"Stay cool," Boardman advised. "If necessary, we can get you out of that ourselves. It's important to humour Muller in everything you can until you've got real rapport with him. If you hear me, touch your right hand to your chin."

Rawlins touched his right hand to his chin.

Muller said, "That was pretty brave of you, Ned. Or stupid. I'm sometimes not sure if there's a distinction. But I'm grateful, anyway. I had to know about those cages."

"Glad to have been of assistance. You see, human beings aren't all that monstrous."

"Not consciously. It's the sludge inside that's ugly. Here, let me remind you." He approached the cage and put his hands on the smooth bars, white as bone. Rawlins felt the emanation intensify. "That's what's under the skull. I've never really felt it myself, of course. I extrapolate it from the response of others. It must be foul."

"I could get used to it," Rawlins said. He sat down cross-legged. "Did you make any attempt to have it undone when you returned to Earth from Beta Hydri IV?"

"I talked to the shape-up boys. They couldn't begin to figure out what changes had been made in my neural flow, and so they couldn't begin to figure out how to fix things. Nice?"

"How long did you stay?"

"A few months. Long enough to discover that there wasn't one human being I knew who didn't turn green after a few minutes of close exposure to me. I started to stew in self-pity, and in self-loathing, which is about the same thing. I was going to kill myself, you know, to put the world out of its misery."

Rawlins said, "I don't believe that. Some men just aren't capable of suicide. You're one who isn't."

"So I discovered, and thank you. I didn't kill myself, you notice. I tried some fancy drugs, and then I tried drink, and then I tried living dangerously. And at the end of it I was still alive. I was in and out of four neuropsychiatric wards in a single month. I tried wearing a padded lead helmet to shield the thought radiations. It was like trying to catch neutrinos in a bucket. I caused a panic in a licensed house on Venus. All the girls stampeded out stark naked once the screaming began." Muller spat. "You know, I could always take society or leave it. When I was among people I was happy, I was cordial, I had the social graces. I wasn't a slick sunny article like you, all overflowing with kindness and nobility, but I interacted with others. I related, I got along. Then I could go on a trip for a year and a half and not see or speak to anyone, and that was all right too. But once I found out that I was shut off from society for good, I discovered that I had needed it after all. But that's over. I outgrew the need, boy.

I can spend a hundred years alone and never miss one soul. I've trained myself to see humanity as humanity sees me—something sickening, a damp hunkering crippled thing best avoided. To hell with you all. I don't owe any of you anything, love included. I have no obligations. I could leave you to rot in that cage, Ned, and never feel upset about it. I could pass that cage twice a day and smile at your skull. It isn't that I hate you, either you personally or the whole galaxy full of your kind. It's simply that I despise you. You're nothing to me. Less than nothing. You're dirt. I know you now, and you know me."

"You speak as if you belong to an alien race," Rawlins said in wonder.

"No. I belong to the human race. I'm the most human being there is, because I'm the only one who can't hide his humanity. You feel it? You pick up the ugliness? What's inside me is also inside you. Go to the Hydrans and they'll help you liberate it, and then people will run from you as they run from me. I speak for man. I tell the truth. I'm the skull beneath the face, boy. I'm the hidden intestines. I'm all the garbage we pretend isn't there, all the filthy animal stuff, the lusts, the little hates, the sicknesses, the envies. And I'm the one who posed as a god. *Hybris.* I was reminded of what I really am."

Rawlins said quietly, "Why did you decide to come to Lemnos?"

"A man named Charles Boardman put the idea into my head."

Rawlins recoiled in surprise at the mention of the name. Muller said, "You know him?"

"Well, yes. Of course. He—he's a very important man in the government."

"You might say that. It was Boardman who sent me to Beta Hydri IV, you know? Oh, he didn't trick me into it, he didn't have to persuade me in any of his slippery ways. He knew me well enough. He simply played on my ambitions. There's a world there with aliens on it, he said, and we want a man to visit it. Probably a suicide mission, but it would be man's first contact with another intelligent species, and are you interested? So of course I went. He knew I couldn't resist something like that. And afterwards, when I came back *this* way, he tried to duck me a while—either because he couldn't abide being near me or because he couldn't abide his own guilt. And finally I caught up with him and I said, look at me, Charles, this is how I am now, where can I go, what shall I do? I got up close to him. This far away. His face changed colour. He had to take pills. I could see the nausea in his eyes. And he reminded me about the maze on Lemnos."

"Why?"

"He offered it as a place to hide. I don't know if he was being kind or cruel. I suppose he thought I'd be killed on my way into the maze—a decent finish for my sort of chap, or at any rate better than taking a gulp of carniphage and melting down a sewer. But of course I told Boardman I wouldn't think of it. I wanted to cover my trail. I blew up and insisted that the last thing in the world I'd do was come here. Then I spent a month on the skids in Under New Orleans, and when I surfaced again I rented a ship and came here. Using maximum diversionary tactics to ensure that nobody found out my true destination. Boardman was right. This was the place to come."

Rawlins said, "How did you get inside the maze?"

"Through sheer bad luck."

"*Bad* luck?"

"I was trying to die in a blaze of glory," said Muller. "I didn't give a damn if I survived the maze or not. I just plunged right in and headed for the middle."

"I can't believe that!"

"Well, it's true, more or less. The trouble was, Ned, I'm a survival type. It's an innate gift, maybe even something paranormal. I have unusual reflexes. I have a kind of sixth sense, as they say. Also my urge to stay alive is well developed. Besides that, I had mass detectors and some other useful equipment. So I came into the maze, and whenever I saw a corpse lying about I looked a little sharper than usual, and I stopped and rested when I felt my visualization of the place beginning to waver. I fully expected to be killed in Zone H. I *wanted* it. But it was my luck to make it where everybody else failed because I didn't care one way or the other, I suppose. The element of tension was removed. I moved like a cat, everything twitching at once, and I got past the tough parts of the maze somehow, much to my disappointment, and here I am."

"Have you ever gone outside it?"

"No. Now and then I go as far as Zone E, where your friends are. Twice I've been to F. Mostly I remain in the three inner zones. I've furnished things quite nicely for myself. I have a radiation locker for my meat supply, and a building I use as my library, and a place where I keep my woman cubes, and I do some taxidermy in one of the other buildings. I hunt quite a lot, also. And I examine the maze and try to analyse its workings. I've dictated several cubes of memoirs on my findings. I bet you archaeologist fellows would love to run through those cubes."

"I'm sure we'd learn a great deal from them," Rawlins said.

"I know you would. I'd destroy them before I'd let any of you see them. Are you getting hungry, boy?"

"A little."

"Don't go away. I'll bring you some lunch."

Muller strode towards the nearby buildings and disappeared. Rawlins said quietly, "This is awful, Charles. He's obviously out of his mind."

"Don't be sure of it," Boardman replied. "No doubt nine years of isolation can have effects on a man's stability, and Muller wasn't all that stable the last time I saw him. But he may be playing a game with you—pretending to be crazy to test your good faith."

"And if he isn't?"

"In terms of what we want from him, it doesn't matter in the slightest if he's insane. It might even help."

"I don't understand that."

"You don't need to," said Boardman evenly. "Just relax. You're doing fine so far."

Muller returned, carrying a platter of meat and a handsome crystal beaker of water. "Best I can offer," he said, pushing a chunk of meat between the bars. "A local beast.

You eat solid food, don't you?"

"Yes."

"At your age, I guess you would. What did you say you were, twenty-five?"

"Twenty-three."

"That's even worse." Muller gave him the water. It had an agreeable flavour, or lack of flavour. Muller sat quietly before the cage, eating. Rawlins noticed that the effect of his emanation no longer seemed so disturbing, even at a range of less than five metres. Obviously one builds a tolerance to it, he thought. If one wants to make the attempt.

Rawlins said, after a while, "Would you come out and meet my companions in a few days?"

"Absolutely not."

"They'd be eager to talk to you."

"I have no interest in talking to them. I'd sooner talk to wild beasts."

"You talk to me," Rawlins pointed out.

"For the novelty of it. And because your father was a good friend. And because, as human beings go, boy, you're reasonably acceptable. But I don't want to be thrust into any miscellaneous mass of bug-eyed archaeologists."

"Possibly meet two or three of them," Rawlins suggested. "Get used to the idea of being among people again."

"No."

"I don't see—"

Muller cut him off. "Wait a minute. *Why* should I get used to the idea of being among people again?"

Rawlins said uneasily, "Well, because there are people here, because it's not a good idea to get too isolated from—"

"Are you planning some sort of trick? Are you going to catch me and pull me out of this maze? Come on, come on, boy, what's in back of that little mind of yours? What motive do you have for softening me up for human contact?"

Rawlins faltered. In the awkward silence Boardman spoke quickly, supplying the guile he lacked, prompting him Rawlins listened and did his best.

He said, "You're making me out to be a real schemer, Dick But I swear to you I've got nothing sinister in mind. I admit

I've been softening you up a little, jollying you, trying to make friends with you, and I guess I'd better tell you why."

"I guess you'd better!"

"It's for the archaeological survey's sake. We can spend only a few weeks here. You've been here—what is it, nine years? You know so much about this place, Dick, and I think it's unfair of you to keep it to yourself. So what I was hoping, I guess, was that I could get you to ease up, first become friendly with me, and then maybe come to Zone E, talk to the others, answer their questions, explain what you know about the maze—"

"*Unfair* to keep it to myself?"

"Well, yes. To hide knowledge is a sin."

"Is it fair of mankind to call me unclean, and run away from me?"

"That's a different matter," Rawlins said. "It's beyond all fairness. It's a condition you have—an unfortunate condition that you didn't deserve, and everyone is quite sorry that it came upon you, but on the other hand, you surely must realize that from the viewpoint of other human beings it's rather difficult to take a detached attitude towards your —your—"

"Towards my stink," Muller supplied. "All right. It's rather difficult to stand my presence. Therefore I willingly refrain from inflicting it upon your friends. Get it out of your head that I'm going to speak to them or sip tea with them or have anything at all to do with them. I have separated myself from the human race and I stay separated. And it's irrelevant that I've granted you the privilege of bothering me. Also, while I'm instructing you, I want to remind you that my unfortunate condition was not undeserved. I earned it by poking my nose into places where I didn't belong, and by thinking I was superhuman for being able to go to such places. *Hybris*. I told you the word."

Boardman continued to instruct him. Rawlins, with the sour taste of lies on his tongue, went on, "I can't blame you for being bitter, Dick. But I still think it isn't right for you to withhold information from us. I mean, look back on your own exploring days. If you landed on a planet, and someone had vital information you had come to find, wouldn't you make every effort to get that information—even though the other person had certain private problems which—"

"I'm sorry," said Muller frostily, "I'm beyond caring," and he walked away, leaving Rawlins alone in the cage with two chunks of meat and the nearly empty beaker of water.

When Muller was out of sight Boardman said, "He's a touchy one, all right. But I didn't expect sweetness from him. You're getting to him, Ned. You're just the right mixture of guile and *naïveté*."

"And I'm in a cage."

"That's no problem. We can send a drone to release you if the cage doesn't open by itself soon."

"Muller isn't going to work out," Rawlins murmured. "He's full of hate. It trickles out of him everywhere. We'll never get him to co-operate. I've never seen such hate in one man."

"You don't know what hate is," said Boardman. "And neither does he. I tell you everything is moving well. There are bound to be some setbacks, but the fact that he's talking to you at all is the important thing. He doesn't *want* to be full of hate. Give him half a chance to get off his frozen position and he will."

"When will you send the probe to release me?"

"Later," said Boardman. "If we have to."

Muller did not return. The afternoon grew darker and the air became chilly. Rawlins huddled uncomfortably in the cage. He tried to imagine this city when it had been alive, when this cage had been used to display prisoners captured in the maze. In the eye of his mind he saw a throng of the city builders, short and thick, with dense coppery fur and greenish skin, swinging their long arms and pointing towards the cage. And in the cage huddled a thing like a giant scorpion with waxy claws that scratched at the stone paving blocks and fiery eyes, and a savage tail that awaited anyone who came too close. Harsh music sounded through the city. Alien laughter. The warm musky reek of the city-builders. Children spitting at the thing in the cage. Their spittle like flame. Bright moonlight, dancing shadows. A trapped creature hideous and malevolent, lonely for its own kind, its hive on a world of Alphecca or Markab, where tailed waxy things moved in shining tunnels. For days the city-builders came, mocked, reproached. The creature in the cage grew sick of their massive bodies and their intertwining spidery fingers, of their flat faces and ugly tusks. And a day came when the floor of the maze gave way, for they were tired of the outworlder captive, and down he went, tail lashing furiously, down into a pit of knives.

It was night. Rawlins had not heard from Boardman for several hours. He had not seen Muller since early afternoon. Animals were prowling the plaza, mostly small ones, all teeth and claws. Rawlins had come unarmed today. He was ready to trample on any beast that slipped between the bars of his cage.

Hunger and cold assailed him. He searched the darkness for Muller. This had ceased to be a joke.

"Can you hear me?" he said to Boardman.

"We're going to get you out soon."

"Yes, but *when*?"

"We sent a probe in, Ned."

"It shouldn't take more than fifteen minutes for a probe to reach me. These zones aren't hazardous."

Boardman paused. "Muller intercepted the probe and destroyed it an hour ago."

"Why didn't you tell me that?"

"We're sending several drones at once," Boardman told him. "Muller's bound to overlook at least one of them. Everything's perfectly all right, Ned. You're in no danger."

"Until something happens," Rawlins said gloomily.

But he did not press the point. Cold, hungry, he slouched against the wall and waited. He saw a small lithe beast stalk and kill a much bigger animal a hundred metres away in the plaza. He watched scavengers scurrying in to rip away slabs of bloody meat. He listened to the sounds of rending and tearing. His view was partially obstructed, and he craned his neck to search for the drone probe that would set him free. No probe appeared.

He felt like a sacrificial victim, staked out for the kill.

The scavengers had finished their work. They came padding across the plaza towards him—little weasel-shaped beasts with big tapering heads and paddle-shaped paws from which yellow recurving claws protruded. Their eyes were red in yellow fields. They studied him with interest, solemnly, thoughtfully. Blood, thick and purplish, was smeared over their muzzles.

They drew nearer. A long narrow snout intruded between two bars of his cage. Rawlins kicked at it. The snout withdrew. To his left, another jutted through. Then there were three snouts.

And then the scavengers began slipping into the cage on all sides.

CHAPTER NINE

BOARDMAN HAD established a comfortable little nest for himself in the Zone F camp. At his age he offered no apologies. He had never been a Spartan, and now, as the price he exacted for making these strenuous and risky journeys, he carried his pleasures around with him. Drones had fetched his belongings from the ship. Under the milky-white curve of the extrusion dome he had carved a private sector with radiant heating, glow-drapes, a gravity suppressor, even a liquor console. Brandy and other delights were never far away. He slept on a soft inflatable mattress covered with a thick red quilt inlaid with heater strands. He knew that the other men in the camp, getting along on far less, bore him no resentment. They expected Charles Boardman to live well wherever he was.

Greenfield entered. "We've lost another drone, sir," he said crisply. "That leaves three in the inner zones."

Boardman flipped the ignition cap on a cigar. He sucked fumes a moment, crossed and uncrossed his legs, exhaled, smiled. "Is Muller going to get those too?"

"I'm afraid so. He knows the access routes better than we do. He's covering them all."

"And you haven't sent any drones in through routes we haven't charted?"

"Two, sir. Lost them both."

"Umm. We'd better send out a great many probes at once, then, and hope we can slip at least one of them past Muller. That boy is getting annoyed at being caged. Change the programme, will you? The brain can manage diversionary tactics, if it's told. Say, twenty probes entering simultaneously."

"We have only three left," Greenfield said.

Boardman bit convulsively into his cigar. "Three here in the camp, or three altogether?"

"Three in camp. Five more outside the maze. They're working their way inward now."

"Who allowed this to happen? Call Hosteen! Get those templates working! I want fifty drones built by morning! No, make it eighty! Of all the stupidity, Greenfield!"

"Yes, sir."

"Get out!"

"Yes, sir."

Boardman puffed furiously. He dialled for brandy, the thick, rich, viscous stuff made by the Prolepticalist Fathers on Deneb XIII. The situation was growing infuriating. He knocked back half a snifter of the brandy, gasped, filled the glass again. He knew that he was in danger of losing his perspective—the worst of sins. The delicacy of this assignment was getting to him. All these mincing steps, the tiny complications, the painstaking edgings towards and away from the goal. Rawlins in the cage. Rawlins and his moral qualms. Muller and his neurotic world-outlook. The little beasts that nipped at your heels here and thoughtfully eyed your throat. The traps these demons had built. And the waiting extragalactics, saucer-eyed, radio-sensed, to whom even a Charles Boardman was no more than an insensate vegetable. Doom overhanging all. Irritably Boardman stubbed out his cigar, and immediately stared at its unfinished length in astonishment. The ignition cap would not work a second time. He leaned forward, got a beam of infrared from the room generator, and kindled it once more, puffing energetically until it was lit. With a petulant gesture of his hand Boardman reactivated his communication link with Ned Rawlins.

The screen showed him moonlight, curving bars, and small furry snouts bristling with teeth.

"Ned?" he said. "Charles here. We're getting you those drones, boy. We'll have you out of that stupid cage in five minutes, do you hear, five minutes!"

2

Rawlins was very busy.

It seemed almost funny. There was no end to the supply of the little beasts. They came nosing through the bars two and three at a time, weasels, ferrets, minks, stoats, whatever they were, all teeth and eyes. But they were scavengers, not killers. God knew what drew them to the cage. They clustered about him, brushing his ankles with their coarse fur, pawing him, slicing through his skin with their claws, biting his shins.

He trampled them. He learned very quickly that a booted foot placed just behind the head could snap a spinal column quickly and effectively. Then, with a swift kick, he could sweep his victim into a corner of the cage, where others would pounce upon it at once. Cannibals, too. Rawlins developed a rhythm of it. Turn, stomp, kick. Turn, stomp, kick. Turn, stomp, kick. Crunch. Crunch. Crunch.

They were cutting him up badly, though.

For the first five minutes he scarcely had time to pause for breath. Turn. Stomp. Kick. He took care of at least twenty of them in that time. Against the far side of the cage a heap of ragged little corpses had risen, with their comrades nosing around hunting for the tender morsels. At last a moment came when all the scavengers currently inside the cage were busy with their fallen cohorts, and no more lurked outside. Rawlins had a momentary respite. He seized a bar with one hand and lifted his left leg to examine the miscellany of cuts, scratches, and bites. Do they give a posthumous Stellar Cross if you die of galactic rabies, he wondered? His leg was bloody from the knee down, and the wounds, though not deep, were hot and painful. Suddenly he discovered why the scavengers had come to him. While he paused he had time to inhale, and he smelled the ripe fragrance of rotting meat. He could almost visualize it: a great bestial corpse, split open at the belly to expose red sticky organs, big black flies circling overhead, perhaps a maggot or two circumnavigating the mound of flesh—

Nothing was rotting in here. The dead scavengers hadn't had time to go bad; little was left of most of them but picked bones by now anyway.

Rawlins realized that it must be some sensory delusion:

an olfactory trap touched off by the cage, evidently. The cage was broadcasting the stink of decay. Why? Obviously to lure that pack of little weasels inside. A refined form of torture. He wondered if Muller had somehow been behind it, going off to a nearby control centre to set up the scent.

He had no further time for contemplation. A fresh battalion of beasts was scurrying across the plaza towards the cage. These looked slightly larger, although not so large that they would not fit between the bars, and their fangs had an ugly gleam in the moonlight. Rawlins hastily stomped three of the snuffling, gorging cannibals still alive in his cage and, in a wondrous burst of inspiration, stuffed them through the bars, giving them a wristflip that tossed them eight or ten metres outside the cage. Good. The newcomers halted, skidding, and began at once to pounce on the twitching and not quite dead bodies that landed before them. Only a few of the scavengers bothered to enter the cage, and these came spaced widely enough so that Rawlins had a chance to trample each in turn and toss it out to feed the onrushing horde. At that rate, he thought, if only new ones would stop coming he could get rid of them all.

New ones finally did stop coming. He had killed seventy or eighty by this time. The stink of raw blood overlaid the synthetic stench of rot; his legs arched from all the carnage, and his brain was orbiting dizzyingly. But at length the night grew peaceful once more. Bodies, some clad in fur, some just a framework of bone, lay strewn in a wide arc before the cage. A thick, deep-hued puddle of mingled bloods spread over a dozen square metres. The last few survivors, stuffed on their gluttony, had gone slinking away without even trying to harass the occupant of the cage. Weary, drained, close to laughter and close to tears, Rawlins clung to the bars and did not look down at his throbbing blood-soaked legs. He felt the fire rising in them. He imagined alien microorganisms launching their argosies in his bloodstream. A bloated purpling corpse by morning, a martyr to Charles Boardman's over-reaching deviousness. What an idiot's move to step into the cage! What a doltish way to win Muller's trust!

Yet the cage had its uses, Rawlins realized suddenly.

Three bulky brutes paraded towards him from different directions. They had the stride of lions, but the swinishness of boars: low-slung sharp-backed creatures, 100 kilograms or so, with long pyramidal heads, slavering thin-lipped mouths, and tiny squinting eyes arranged in two sets of two on either side just in front their ragged droopy ears. Curving tusks jutted down and intersected smaller and sharper canine teeth that rose from powerful jaws.

The trio of uglies inspected one another suspiciously, and performed a complex series of loping movements which neatly demonstrated the three-body problem as they executed circular interlocking trots by way of staking out territory. They rooted about a bit in the heap of scavenger corpses, but clearly they were no scavengers themselves; they were looking for living meat, and their disdain for the broken cannibalized little bodies was evident. When they had completed their inspection they swung about to stare at Rawlins, standing at a three-quarters-profile angle so that each of them had one pair of eyes looking at him straight on. Rawlins was grateful for the security of his cage. He would not care to be outside, unprotected and exhausted, with these three cruising the city for their dinner.

At that moment, of course, the bars of the cage silently began to retract.

3

Muller, arriving just then, took in the whole scene. He paused only briefly to admire the seductive vanishing of the cage into the recessed slots. He contemplated the three hungry pigs and the dazed, bloody form of Rawlins standing suddenly exposed before them. "Get down!" Muller yelled.

Rawlins got down by taking four running steps to the left, slipping on the blood-slicked pavement, and skidding into a heap of small cadavers at the edge of the street. In the same moment Muller fired, not bothering with keying in the manual sighting since these were not edible animals. Three quick bolts brought the pigs down. They did not move again. Muller started to go to Rawlins, but then one of the robots

135

from the camp in Zone F appeared, gliding cheerfully towards them. Muller cursed softly. He pulled the destructor globe from his pocket and aimed the window at the robot. The probe turned a mindless blank face at him as he fired.

The robot disintegrated. Rawlins had managed to get up. "You shouldn't have blasted it," he said woozily. "It was just coming to help."

"No help was needed," said Muller. "Can you walk?"

"I think so."

"How badly are you hurt?"

"I've been chewed on, that's all. It isn't as bad as it looks."

"Come with me," Muller said. Already more scavengers were filing through the plaza, drawn by the mysterious tele-graphy of blood. Small, toothy things were getting down to serious work on the trio of fallen boars. Rawlins looked un-steady; he seemed to be talking to himself. Forgetting his own emanation, Muller seized him by the arm. Rawlins winced and twitched away, and then, as if repenting the appearance of rudeness, gave Muller his arm again. They crossed the plaza together. Rawlins was shaking, and Muller did not know whether he was more disturbed by his narrow escape or by the jangling propinquity of an unshielded mind.

"In here," Muller said roughly.

They stepped into the hexagonal cell where he kept his diagnostat. Muller sealed the door, and Rawlins sank down limply on the bare floor. His blond hair was pasted by perspiration to his forehead. His eyes were moving jerkily, the pupils dilated.

Muller said, "How long were you under attack?"

"Fifteen, twenty minutes. I don't know. There must have been fifty or a hundred of them. I kept breaking their backs. A quick crunching sound, you know, like splitting twigs. And then the cage went away." Rawlins laughed wildly. "That was the best part. I had just finished smashing up all those little bastards and was catching my breath, and then the three big monsters came along, and so naturally the cage vanished and—"

"Easy," Muller said, "you're talking so fast I can't follow everything. Can you get those boots off?"

136

"What's left of them."

"Yes. Get them off and we'll patch those legs of yours. Lemnos has no shortage of infectious bacteria. And protozoa, and for all I know algae and trypanosomes, and more."

Rawlins picked at the catches. "Can you help me? I'm afraid that I can't—"

"You won't like it if I come any closer," Muller warned.

"To hell with that!"

Muller shrugged. He approached Rawlins and manipulated the broken and bent snaps of the boots. The metal chasing was scarred by tiny teeth; so were the boots themselves, and so were the legs. In a few moments Rawlins was out of his boots and leggings. He lay stretched out on the floor, grimacing and trying to look heroic. His legs were in bad shape, though none of the wounds seemed really serious; it was just that there were so many of them. Muller got the diagnostat going. The lamps glowed and the receptor slot beckoned.

"It's an old model," Rawlins said. "I'm not sure what to do."

"Stick your legs in front of the scanner."

Rawlins swivelled about. A blue light played on his wounds. In the bowels of the diagnostat things chuttered and clicked. A swab came forth on a jointed arm and ran deftly and lightly up his left leg to a point just above the knee. The machine engulfed the bloody swab and began to digest it back to its component molecules while a second swab emerged to clean Rawlins' other leg. Rawlins bit his lip. He was getting a coagulant as well as a cleanser so that when the swabs had done their work all blood was gone and the hallow gouges and rips were revealed. It still looked pretty bad, Muller thought, though not as grim as before.

The diagnostat produced an ultrasonic node and injected a golden fluid into Rawlins' rump. Pain-damper, Muller guessed. A second injection, deep amber, was probably some kind of all-purpose antibiotic to ward off infection. Rawlins grew visibly less tense. Now a variety of arms sprang forward from various sectors of the device, inspecting Rawlins' lesions in detail and scanning them for necessary repairs. There was a humming sound and three sharp clicks. Then the diagnostat began to seal the wounds, clamping them firmly.

"Lie still," Muller told him. "You'll be all right in a couple of minutes."

"You shouldn't be doing this," said Rawlins. "We have our own medical supplies back in camp. You must be running short on necessities. All you had to do was let the drone probe take me back to my camp, and—"

"I don't want those robots crawling around in here. And the diagnostat has at least a fifty-year supply of usefuls. I don't get sick often. It can synthesize most of what it's ever going to need for me. So long as I feed it protoplasm from time to time, it can do the rest."

"At least let us send you replacements for some of the rare drugs."

"Not necessary. No charity wanted. Ah! There, it's done with you. Probably you won't even have scars."

The machine released Rawlins, who swung away from it and looked up at Muller. The wildness was gone from the boy's face now. Muller lounged against the wall, rubbing his shoulderblades against the angle where two faces of the hexagon met, and said, "I didn't think that you'd be attacked by beasts or I wouldn't have left you alone so long. You aren't armed?"

"No."

"Scavengers don't bother living things. What made them go after you?"

"The cage did," Rawlins said. "It began to broadcast the smell of rotting flesh. A lure. Suddenly they were crawling all over me. I thought they'd eat me alive."

Muller grinned. "Interesting. So the cage is programmed as a trap too. We get some useful information out of your little predicament, then. I can't tell you how interested I am in those cages. In every part of this weird environment of mine. The aqueduct. The calendar pylons. The streetcleaning apparatus. I'm grateful to you for helping me learn a little."

"I know someone else who has that attitude," said Rawlins. "That it doesn't matter what the risk or cost so long as you collect some useful data out of the experience. Board—"

He cut the word short with a crisp biting gesture.

"Who?"

"Bordoni," Rawlins said. "Emilio Bordoni, my epistemology professor at college. He gave this marvellous course. Actually it was applied hermeneutics, a course in how to learn."

"That's heuristics," said Muller.

"Are you sure? I have a distinct impression—"

"It's wrong," said Muller. "You're talking to an authority. Hermeneutics is the art of interpretation. Originally Scriptural interpretation but now applying to all communications functions. Your father would have known that. My mission to the Hydrans was an experiment in applied hermeneutics. It wasn't successful."

"Heuristics. Hermeneutics." Rawlins laughed. "Well, anyway, I'm glad to have helped you learn something about the cages. My heuristic good deed. Am I excused from the next round?"

"I suppose," Muller said. Somehow an odd feeling of good will had come over him. He had almost forgotten how pleasant it was to be able to help another person. Or to enjoy lazy, irrelevant conversation. He said, "Do you drink, Ned?"

"Alcoholic beverages?"

"So I mean."

"In moderation."

"This is our local liqueur," said Muller. "It's produced by gnomes somewhere in the bowels of the planet." He produced a delicate flask and two wide-mouthed goblets. Carefully he tipped about twenty centilitres into each goblet. "I get this in Zone C," he explained, handing Rawlins his drink. "It rises from a fountain. It really ought to be labelled DRINK ME, I guess."

Gingerly Rawlins tasted it. "Strong!"

"About sixty per cent alcohol, yes. Lord knows what the rest of it is, or how it's synthesized or why. I simply accept it. I like the way it manages to be both sweet and gingery at the same time. Its terribly intoxicating, of course. It's intended as another trap, I suppose. You get happily drunk—and then the maze gets you." He raised his goblet amiably.

"Cheers!"

"Cheers!"

They laughed at the archaic toast and drank.

Careful, Dickie, Muller told himself. You're getting down-right sociable with this boy. Remember where you are. And why. What kind of ogre are you, acting this way?

"May I take some of this back to camp with me?" Rawlins asked.

"I suppose so. Why?"

"There's a man there who'd appreciate it. He's a gourmet of sorts. He's travelling with a liquor console that dispenses a hundred different drinks, I imagine, from about forty different worlds. I can't remember the names."

"Anything from Marduk?" Muller asked. "The Deneb worlds? Rigel?"

"I really can't be sure. I mean, I enjoy drinking, but I'm no connoisseur."

"Perhaps this friend of yours would be willing to ex-change—" Muller stopped. "No. No. Forget I said that. I'm not getting into any deals."

"You could come back to camp with me," said Rawlins. "He'd give you the run of the console, I'm sure."

"Very subtle of you. No." Muller glowered at his liqueur. "I won't be eased into it, Ned. I don't want anything to do with the others."

"I'm sorry you feel that way."

"Another drink?"

"No. I'll have to start getting back to camp now. It's late. I wasn't supposed to spend the whole day here, and I'll catch hell for not doing my share of the work."

"You were in the cage most of the day. They can't blame you for that."

"They might. They were complaining a little yesterday. I don't think they want me to visit you."

Muller felt a sudden tightness within.

Rawlins went on, "After the way I kicked away a day's work today I wouldn't be surprised if they refused to let me come in here again. They'll be pretty stuffy about it. I mean, considering that you don't seem very co-operative, they'll regard it as wasted time for me to be paying calls on you when I could be manning the equipment in Zone E or F." Rawlins finished his drink and got to his feet, grunting a little. He looked down at his bare legs. The diagnostat had covered the wounds with a nutrient spray, flesh-coloured; it was almost impossible to tell that his skin had been broken anywhere. Stiffly, he pulled his tattered leggings on. "I won't bother with the boots," he said. "They're in bad shape, and it won't be pleasant trying to get them on. I suppose I can get back to camp barefoot."

"The pavement is very smooth," Muller said.

"You'll give me some of that liqueur for my friend?"

Silently Muller extended the flask, half full.

Rawlins clipped it to his belt. "It was an interesting day. I hope I can come again."

4

Boardman said, as Rawlins limped back towards Zone E, "How are your legs?"

"Tired. They're healing fast. I'll be all right."

"Be careful not to drop that flask."

"Don't worry, Charles. I have it well fastened. I wouldn't deprive you of the experience."

"Ned, listen to me, we did try to get the drones to you. I was watching every terrible minute of it when those animals were attacking you. But there was nothing we could do. Muller was intercepting our probes and knocking them out."

"All right," Rawlins said.

"He's clearly unstable. He wasn't going to let one of those drones into the inner zones."

"All right, Charles, I survived."

Boardman could not let go of it. "It occurred to me that if we hadn't tried to send the drones at all, you would have been better off, Ned. The drones kept Muller busy for a long while. He might have gone back to your cage instead. Let you out. Or killed the animals. He——" Halting, Boardman quirked his lips and denounced himself inwardly for maundering. A sign of age. He felt the folds of flesh at his belly. He needed another shape-up. Bring his age forward to an apparent sixty or so, while actually cutting the physiological deterioration back to biological fifty. Older outside than within. A façade of shrewdness to hide shrewdness.

He said, after a long while, "It seems you and Muller are quite good friends now. I'm pleased. It's coming to be time for you to tempt him out."

"How do I do that?"

"Promise him a cure," Boardman said.

CHAPTER TEN

THEY MET again on the third day afterwards, at midday in Zone B. Muller seemed relieved to see him, which was the idea. Rawlins came diagonally across the oval ball-court, or whatever it was, that lay between two snub-nosed dark blue towers, and Muller nodded. "How are your legs?"

"Doing fine."

"And your friend—he liked the liqueur?"

"He loved it," Rawlins said, thinking of the glow in Boardman's foxy eyes. "He sends back your flask with some special brandy in it and hopes you'll treat him to a second round."

Muller eyed the flask as Rawlins held it forth. "He can go to hell," Muller said coolly. "I won't get into any trades. If you give me that flask I'll smash it."

"Why?"

"Give it here, and I'll show you. No. Wait. Wait. I won't. Here, let me have it."

Rawlins surrendered it. Muller cradled the lovely flask tenderly in both hands, activated the cap, and put it to his lips. "You devils," he said in a soft voice. "What is this, from the monastery on Deneb XIII?"

"He didn't say. He just said you'd like it."

"Devils Temptations. It's a trade, damn you! But only this once. If you show up here again with more liqueur—anything—the elixir of the gods—anything, I'll refuse it. Where have you been all week, anyway?"

"Working, I told you they frowned on my coming to see you."

He missed me, Rawlins thought. Charles is right: I'm getting to him. Why does he have to be such a difficult character?

"Where are they excavating?" Muller asked.

"They aren't excavating at all. They're using sonic probes

143

at the border between Zones E and F, trying to determine the chronology—whether the whole maze was built at once, or in accretive layers out from the middle. What's your opinion, Dick?"

"Go to hell. No free archaeology out of me!" Muller sipped the brandy again. "You're standing pretty close to me, aren't you?"

"Four or five metres, I guess."

"You were closer when you gave me the brandy. Why didn't you look sick? Didn't you feel the effect?"

"I felt it, yes."

"And hid your feelings like the good stoic you are?"

Shrugging, Rawlins said genially, "I guess the effect loses impact on repeated exposure. It's still pretty strong, but not the way it was for me the first day. Have you ever noticed that happening with someone else?"

"There were no repeated exposures with anyone else," said Muller. "Come over here, boy. See the sights. This is my water supply. Quite elegant. This black pipe runs right around Zone B. Onyx, I guess. Semiprecious. Handsome, at any rate." Muller knelt and stroked the aqueduct. "There's a pumping system. Brings up water from some underground aquifer, maybe a thousand kilometres down, I don't know. This planet doesn't have any surface water, does it?"

"It has oceans."

"Aside from—well, whatever. Over here, you see, here's one of the spigots. Every fifty metres. As far as I can tell it's the water supply for the entire city, right here, so perhaps the builders didn't need much water. It couldn't have been very important if they set things up like this. No conduits that I've found. No real plumbing. Thirsty?"

"Not really."

Muller cupped his hand under the ornately engraved spigot, a thing of concentric ridges. Water gushed. Muller took a few quick gulps; the flow ceased the moment the hand was removed from the area below the spigot. A scanning system of some kind, Rawlins thought. Clever. How had it lasted all these millions of years?

"Drink," Muller said. "You may get thirsty later on."

"I can't stay long." But he drank anyway. Afterwards they walked into Zone A, an easy stroll. The cages had closed again; Rawlins saw several of them, and shuddered. He would try no such experiments today. They found benches, slabs of polished stone that curled at the ends into facing seats intended for some species very much broader in the buttock than the usual *H. sapiens*. Sitting like this they could talk at a distance, Rawlins feeling only mild discomfort from Muller's emanation, and yet there was no sensation of separation.

Muller was in a talkative mood.

The conversation was fitful, dissolving every now and then into an acid spray of anger or self-pity, but most of the time Muller remained calm and even charming—an older man clearly enjoying the company of a younger one, the two of them exchanging opinions, experiences, scraps of philosophy. Muller spoke a good deal about his early career, the planets he had seen, the delicate negotiations on behalf of Earth with the frequently prickly colony-worlds. He mentioned Boardman's name quite often; Rawlins kept his face studiously blank. Muller's attitude towards Boardman seemed to be one of deep admiration shot through with furious loathing. He could not forgive Boardman, apparently, for having played on his own weaknesses in getting him to go to the Hydrans. Not a rational attitude, Rawlins thought. Given Muller's trait of overweening curiosity, he would have fought for that assignment, Boardman or no, risks or no.

"And what about you?" Muller asked finally. "You're brighter than you pretend to be. Hampered a little by your shyness, but plenty of brains, carefully hidden behind college-boy virtues. What do you want for yourself, Ned? What does archaeology give you?"

Rawlins looked him straight in the eyes. "A chance to recapture a million pasts. I'm as greedy as you are. I want to know how things happened, how they got this way. Not just on Earth or in the System. Everywhere."

"Well spoken!"

I thought so too, Rawlins thought, hoping Boardman was

pleased by his newfound eloquence.

He said, "I suppose I could have gone in for diplomatic service, the way you did. Instead I chose this. I think it'll work out. There's so much to discover, here and everywhere else. We've only begun to look."

"The ring of dedication is in your voice."

"I suppose."

"I like to hear that sound. It reminds me of the way I used to talk."

Rawlins said, "Just so you don't think I'm hopelessly pure I ought to say that it's personal curiosity that moves me on, more than abstract love of knowledge."

"Understandable. Forgivable. We're not too different, really. Allowing for forty-odd years between us. Don't worry so much about your motives, Ned. Go to the stars, see, do. Enjoy. Eventually life will smash you, the way it's smashed me, but that's far off. Sometime, never, who knows? Forget about that."

"I'll try," Rawlins said.

He felt the warmth of the man now, the reaching out of genuine sympathies. There was still that carrier wave of nightmare, though, the unending broadcast out of the mucky depths of the soul, attenuated at this distance but unmistakable. Imprisoned by his pity, Rawlins hesitated to say what it now was time to say. Boardman prodded him irritably. "Go *on,* boy! Slip it in!"

"You look very far away," Muller said.

"Just thinking how—how sad it is that you won't trust us at all, that you have such a negative attitude towards humanity."

"I come by it honestly."

"You don't need to spend the rest of your life in this maze, though. There's a way out."

"Garbage."

"Listen to me," Rawlins said. He took a deep breath and flashed his quick, transparent grin. "I talked about your case to our expedition medic. He's studied neurosurgery. He knew all about you. He says there's now a way to fix what you have. Recently developed, the last couple of years. It—

shuts off the broadcast, Dick. He said I should tell you. We'll take you back to Earth. For the operation, Dick. The operation. The cure."

2

The sharp glittering barbed word came swimming along on the breast of a torrent of bland sounds and speared him in the gut. *Cure!* He stared. There was reverberation from the looming dark buildings. *Cure. Cure. Cure.* Muller felt the poisonous temptation gnawing at his liver. "No," he said. "That's garbage. A cure's impossible."

"How can you be so sure?"

"I know."

"Science progresses in nine years. They understand how the brain works, now. Its electrical nature. What they did, they built a tremendous simulation in one of the lunar labs— oh, a few years ago, and they ran it all through from start to finish. As a matter of fact I'm sure they're desperate to have you back, because you prove all their theories. In your present condition. And by operating on you, reversing your broadcast, they'll demonstrate that they were right. All you have to do is come back with us."

Muller methodically popped his knuckles. "Why didn't you mention this earlier?"

"I didn't know a thing about it."

"Of course."

"Really. We didn't expect to be finding you here, you realize. At first nobody was too sure who you were, why you were here. I explained it. And then the medic remembered that there was this treatment. What's wrong—don't you believe me?"

"You look so angelic," Muller said. "Those sweet blue eyes and that golden hair. What's your game, Ned? Why are you reeling off all this nonsense?"

Rawlins reddened. "It isn't nonsense!"

"I don't believe you. And I don't believe in your cure."

"It's your privilege. But you'll be the loser if—"

"Don't threaten me!"

147

"I'm sorry."

There was a long, sticky silence.

Muller revolved a maze of thoughts. To leave Lemnos? To have the curse lifted? To hold a woman in his arms again? Breasts like fire against his skin? Lips? Thighs? To rebuild his career. To reach across the heavens once more? To shuck nine years of anguish? To believe? To go? To submit?

"No," he said carefully. "There is no cure for what I have."

"You keep saying that. But you can't know."

"It doesn't fit the pattern. I believe in destiny, boy. In compensating tragedy. In the overthrow of the proud. The gods don't deal out temporary tragedies. They don't take back their punishments after a few years. Oedipus didn't get his eyes back. Or his mother. They didn't let Prometheus off the rock. They—"

"You aren't living a Greek play," Rawlins told him. "This is the real world. The patterns don't always fall neatly. Maybe the gods have decided that you've suffered enough. And so long as we're having a literary discussion—they forgave Orestes, didn't they? So why isn't nine years here enough for you?"

"*Is* there a cure?"

"The medic says there is."

"I think you're lying to me, boy."

Rawlins glanced away. "What do I have to gain by lying?"

"I can't guess."

"All right, I'm lying," Rawlins said brusquely. "There's no way to help you. Let's talk about something else. Why don't you show me the fountain where that liqueur rises?"

"It's in Zone C," said Muller. "I don't feel like going there just now. Why did you tell me that story if it wasn't true?"

"I said we'd change the subject."

"Let's assume for the moment that it *is* true," Muller persisted. "That if I go back to Earth I can be cured. I want to let you know that I'm not interested, not even with a guarantee. I've seen Earthmen in their true nature. They kicked me when I was down. Not sporting, Ned. They stink. They

148

reek. They gloried in what had happened to me."

"That isn't so!"

"What do you know? You were a child. Even more then than now. They treated me as filth because I showed them what was inside themselves. A mirror for their dirty souls. Why should I go back to them now? Why do I need them? Worms. Pigs. I saw them as they really are, those few months I was on earth after Beta Hydri IV. The look in the eyes, the nervous smile as they back away from me. Yes, Mr. Muller. Of course, Mr. Muller. Just don't come too close, Mr. Muller. Boy, come by here some time at night and let me show you the constellations as seen from Lemnos. I've given them my own names. There's the Dagger, a long keen one. It's about to be thrust into the Back. Then there's the Shaft. And you can see the Ape, too, and the Toad. They interlock. The same star is in the forehead of the Ape and the left eye of the Toad. That star is Sol, my friend. An ugly little yellow star, the colour of thin vomit. Whose planets are populated by ugly little people who have spread like trickling urine over the whole universe."

"Can I say something that might offend you?" Rawlins asked.

"You can't offend me. But you can try."

"I think your outlook is distorted. You've lost your perspective, all these years here."

"No. I've learned how to see for the first time."

"You're blaming humanity for being human. It's not easy to accept someone like you. If you were sitting here in my place, and I in yours, you'd understand that. It hurts to be near you. *It hurts.* Right now I feel pain in every nerve. If I came closer I'd feel like crying. You can't expect people to adjust quickly to somebody like that. Not even your loved ones could—"

"I had no loved ones."

"You were married."

"Terminated."

"Liaisons, then."

"They couldn't stand me when I came back."

"Friends?"

"They ran," Muller said. "On all six legs they scuttled away from me."

"You didn't give them time."

"Time enough."

"No," Rawlins persisted. He shifted about uneasily on the chair. "Now I'm going to say something that will really hurt you, Dick. I'm sorry, but I have to. What you're telling me is the kind of stuff I heard in college. Sophomore cynicism. The world is despicable, you say. Evil, evil, evil. You've seen the true nature of mankind, and you don't want to have anything to do with mankind ever again. Everybody talks that way at eighteen. But it's a phase that passes. We get over the confusions of being eighteen, and we see that the world is a pretty decent place, that people try to do their best, that we're imperfect but not loathsome—"

"An eighteen-year-old has no right to those opinions. I do. I come by my hatreds the hard way."

"But why cling to them? You seem to be glorying in your own misery. Break loose! Shake it off! Come back to Earth with us and forget the past. Or at least forgive."

"No forgetting. No forgiving." Muller scowled. A tremor of fear shook him, and he shivered. What if this were true? A genuine cure? Leave Lemnos? He was a trifle embarrassed. They boy had scored a palpable hit with that line about sophomore cynicism. It was. Am I really such a misanthrope? A pose. He forced me to adopt it. Polemic reasons. Now I choke on my own stubborness. But there's no cure. The boy's transparent; he's lying, though I don't know why. He wants to trap me, to get me aboard that ship of theirs. What if it's true? Why not go back? Muller could supply his own answers. It was the fear that held him. To see Earth's billions. To enter the stream of life. Nine years on a desert island and he dreaded to return. He slipped into a pit of depression, recognizing hard truths. The man who would be a god was just a pitiful neurotic now, clinging to his isolation, spitting defiance at a possible rescuer. Sad, Muller thought. Very sad.

Rawlins said, "I can feel the flavour of your thoughts changing."

"You *can*?"

"Nothing specific. But you were angry and bitter before. Now I'm getting something—wistful."

"No one ever told me he could detect meanings," Muller said in wonder. "No one ever said much. Only that it was painful to be near me. Disgusting."

"Why did you go wistful just then, though? If you did. Thinking of Earth?"

"Maybe I was." Muller hastily patched the sudden gap in his armour. His face darkened. He clenched his jaws. He stood up and deliberately approached Rawlins, watching the young man struggling to hide his real feelings of discomfort. Muller said, "I think you'd better get about your archaeologizing now, Ned. Your friends will be angry again."

"I still have some time."

"No, you don't. Go!"

3

Against Charles Boardman's express orders, Rawlins insisted on returning all the way to the Zone F camp that evening. The pretext was that Rawlins had to deliver the new flask of liqueur which he had finally been able to wheedle out of Muller. Boardman wanted one of the other men to pick up the flask, sparing Rawlins from the risks of Zone F's snares. Rawlins needed the direct contact, though. He was badly shaken. His resolve was sagging.

He found Boardman at dinner. A polished dining-board of dark wood mortised with light woods sat before him. Out of elegant stoneware he ate candied fruits, brandied vegetables, meat extracts, pungent juices. A carafe of wine of a deep olive hue was near his fleshy hand. Mysterious pills of several types rested in the shallow pits of an oblong block of black glass; from time to time Boardman popped one into his mouth. Rawlins stood at the sector opening for a long while before Boardman appeared to notice him.

"I told you not to come here, Ned," the old man said finally.

"Muller sends you this." Rawlins put the flask down

beside the carafe of wine.

"We could have talked without this visit."

"I'm tired of that. I needed to see you." Boardman left him standing and did not interrupt his meal. "Charles, I don't think I can keep up the pretence with him."

"You did an excellent job today," said Boardman, sipping his wine. "Quite convincing."

"Yes, I'm learning how to tell lies. But what's the use? You heard him. Mankind disgusts him. He's not going to co-operate once we get him out of the maze."

"He isn't sincere. You said it yourself, Ned. Cheap sophomore cynicism. The man loves mankind. That's why he's so bitter—because his love has turned sour in his mouth. But it hasn't turned to hate. Not really."

"You weren't there, Charles. You weren't talking to him."

"I watched. I listened. And I've known Dick Muller for forty-odd years."

"The last nine years are the ones that count. They've twisted him." Rawlins bent into a crouch to get on Boardman's level. Boardman nudged a candied pear on to his fork, equalized gravity, and flipped it idly towards his mouth. He's intentionally ignoring me, Rawlins thought. He said, "Charles, be serious. I've gone in there and told Muller some monstrous lies. I've offered him a completely fraudulent cure, and he threw it back in my face."

"Saying he didn't believe it existed. But he *does* believe, Ned. He's simply afraid of coming out of hiding."

"Please. Listen. Assume he does come to believe me. Assume he leaves the maze and puts himself in our hands. Then what? Who gets the job of telling him that there isn't any cure, that we've tricked him shamelessly, that we merely want him to be of our ambassador again, to visit a bunch of aliens twenty times as strange and fifty times as deadly as the ones that ruined his life? *I'm* not going to break that news to him!"

"You won't have to, Ned. I'll be the one."

"And how will he react? Are you simply expecting him to smile and bow and say, very clever, Charles, you've done it again? To yield and do whatever you want? No. He couldn't possibly. You can get him out of the maze, maybe, but the very methods you use for getting him out make it inconceivable that he can be of any use to you once he *is* out."

"That isn't necessarily true," said Boardman calmly.

"Will you explain the tactics you propose to use, then, once you've informed him that the cure is a lie and that there's a dangerous new job he has to undertake?"

"I prefer not to discuss future strategy now."

"I resign," Rawlins said.

Boardman had been expecting something like that. A noble gesture; a moment of headstrong defiance; a rush of virtue to the brain. Abandoning now his studied detachment, he looked up, his eyes locking firmly on Rawlins'. Yes, there was strength there. Yes, determination. But not guile. Not yet.

Quietly Boardman said, "You resign? After all your talk of service to mankind? We need you, Ned. You're the indispensable man, our link to Muller."

"My dedication to mankind includes a dedication to Dick Muller," Rawlins said stiffly. "He's part of mankind, whether he thinks so or not. I've already committed a considerable crime against him. If you won't let me in on the rest of this scheme, I'm damned if I'll have any part in it."

"I admire your convictions."

"My resignation still stands."

"I even agree with your position," said Boardman. "I'm not proud of what we must do here. I see it as part of historical necessity—the need for an occasional betrayal for the greater good. I have a conscience too, Ned, an eighty-year-old conscience, very well developed. It doesn't atrophy with age. We just learn to live with its complaints, that's all."

"How are you going to get Muller to co-operate? Drug him? Torture him? Brainblast him?"

"None of those."

"What, then? I'm serious, Charles. My role in this job ends right here unless I know what's ahead."

Boardman coughed, drained his wine, ate a peach, took three pills in quick succession. Rawlins' rebellion had been inevitable, and he was prepared for it, and yet he was annoyed that it had come. Now was the time for calculated risks. He said, "I see that it's time to drop the pretences, then, Ned. I'll tell you what's in store for Dick Muller—but I want you to consider it within the framework of the larger position. Don't forget that the little game we've been playing on this planet isn't simply a matter of private moral postures. At the risk of sounding pretentious, I have to remind you that mankind's fate is at stake."

"I'm listening, Charles."

"Very well. Dick Muller must go to our extragalactic friends and convince them that human beings are indeed an intelligent species. Agreed? He alone is capable of doing this, because of his unique inability to cloak his thoughts."

"Agreed."

"Now, it isn't necessary to convince the aliens that we're good people, or that we're honourable people, or that we're lovable people. Simply that we have minds and can think. That we feel, that we sense, that we are something other than clever machines. For our purposes, it doesn't matter *what* emotions Dick Muller is radiating so long as he's radiating something."

"I begin to see."

"Therefore, once he's out of the maze we can tell him what his assignment is to be. No doubt he'll get angry at our trickery. But beyond his anger he may see where his duty lies. I hope so. You seem to think he won't. But it makes no difference, Ned. He won't be given an option once he leaves his sanctuary. He'll be taken to the aliens and handed over to them to make contact. It's brutal, I know. But necessary."

"His co-operation is irrelevant, then," said Rawlins slowly. "He'll just be dumped. Like a sack."

"A *thinking* sack. As our friends out there will learn."

"I—"

"No, Ned. Don't say anything now. I know what you're thinking. You hate the scheme. You have to. I hate it myself. Just go off, now, and think it over. Examine it from all sides before you come to a decision. If you want out tomorrow, let me know and we'll carry on somehow without you, but promise me you'll sleep on it first. Yes? This is no time for a snap

154

judgment."

Rawlins' face was pale a moment. Then colour flooded into it. He clamped his lips. Boardman smiled benignly. Rawlins clenched his fists, squinted, turned, hastily went out.

A calculated risk.

Boardman took another pill. Then he reached for the flask Muller had sent him. He poured a little. Sweet, gingery, strong. An excellent liqueur. He let it rest a while on his tongue.

CHAPTER ELEVEN

MULLER HAD almost come to like the Hydrans. What he remembered most clearly and most favourably about them was their grace of motion. They seemed virtually to float. The strangeness of their bodies had never bothered him much; he was fond of saying that one did not need to go far from Earth to find the grotesque. Giraffes. Lobsters. Sea anemones. Squids. Camels. Look objectively at a camel and ask yourself what is less strange about its body than about a Hydran's.

He had landed in a damp, dreary part of the planet, a little to the north of its equator, on an amoeboid continent occupied by a dozen large quasicities, each spread out over several thousand square kilometres. His life-support system, specially designed for this mission, was little more than a thin filtration sheet that clung to him like a second skin. It fed air to him through a thousand dialysis plaques. He moved easily if not comfortably within it.

He walked for an hour through a forest of the giant toadstool-like trees before he came upon any of the natives. The trees ran to heights of several hundred metres; perhaps the gravity, five-eighths Earthnorm, had something to do with that. Their curving trunks did not look sturdy. He suspected that an external woody layer no thicker than a fingertip surrounded a broad core of soggy pulp. The cap-like crowns of the trees met in a nearly continuous canopy overhead, cutting almost all light from the forest floor. Since the planet's cloud layer permitted only a hazy pearl-coloured glow to come through, and even that was intercepted by the trees, a maroon darkness prevailed below.

When he encountered the aliens he was surprised to find that they were about three metres tall. Not since childhood had he felt so diminished; he stood ringed by them, straining upward to meet their eyes. Now it was time for his exercise in appled hermeneutics. In a quiet voice he said, "My name is Richard Muller. I come in friendship from the peoples of the Terran Cultural Sphere."

Of course they could not understand that. But they remained motionless. He imagined that their expressions were not unfriendly.

Dropping to his knees, Muller traced the Pythagorean Theorem in the soft moist soil.

He looked up. He smiled. "A basic concept of geometry. A universal pattern of thought."

Their vertical slitlike nostrils flickered slightly. They inclined their heads. He imagined that they were exchanging thoughtful glances. With eyes in a circlet entirely around their heads, they did not need to change posture to do that.

"Let me display some further tokens of our kinship," Muller said to them.

He sketched a line on the ground. A short distance from it he sketched a pair of lines. At a greater distance he drew three lines. He filled in the signs. $I + II = III$.

"Yes?" he said. "We call it addition."

The jointed limbs swayed. Two of his listeners touched arms. Muller remembered how they had obliterated the spying eye as soon as they had discovered it, not hesitating even to examine it. He had been prepared for the same reaction. Instead they were listening. A promising sign. He stood up and pointed to his marks on the ground.

"Your turn," he said. He spoke quite loudly. He smiled quite broadly. "Show me that you understand. Speak to me in the universal language of mathematics."

No response at first.

He pointed again. He gestured at his symbols, then extended his hand, palm upraised, to the nearest Hydran.

After a long pause one of the other Hydrans moved fluidly forward and let one of its globe-like foot-pedestals hover over the lines in the soil. The leg moved lightly and the lines vanished as the alien smoothed the soil.

"All right," said Muller. "Now you draw something."

The Hydran returned to its place in the circle.

"Very well," Muller said. "There's another universal

language. I hope this doesn't offend your ears." He drew a soprano recorder from his pocket and put it between his lips. Playing through the filtration sheet was cumbersome. He caught breath and played a diatonic scale. Their limbs fluttered a bit. They could hear, then, or at any rate could sense vibrations. He shifted to the minor, and gave them another diatonic scale. He tried a chromatic scale. They looked a trifle more agitated. Good for you, he thought. Connoisseurs. Perhaps the whole-tone scale is more in keeping with the cloudiness of this planet, he decided. He played both of them, and gave a bit of Debussy for good measure.

"Does that get to you?" he asked.

They appeared to be conferring.

They walked away from him.

He tried to follow. He was unable to keep up, and soon he lost sight of them in the dark, misty forest; but he persevered, and found them clustered, as if waiting for him, farther on. When he neared them they began to move again. In this way they led him, by fits and starts, into their city.

He subsisted on synthetics. Chemical analysis showed that it would be unwise to try local foods.

He drew the Pythagorean Theorem many times. He sketched a variety of arithmetical processes. He played Schönberg and Bach. He constructed equilateral triangles. He ventured into solid geometry. He sang. He spoke French, Russian, and Mandarin, as well as English, to show them the diversity of human tongues. He displayed a chart of the periodic table. After six months he still knew nothing more about the working of their minds than he had an hour before landing. They tolerated his presence, but they said nothing to him; and when they communicated with one another it was mainly in quick, evanescent gestures, touches of the hand, flickers of the nostrils. They had a spoken language, it seemed, but it was so soft and breathy that he could not begin to distinguish words or even syllables. He recorded whatever he heard, of course.

Eventually they wearied of him and came for him.

He slept.

He did not discover until much later what had been done to him while he slept.

2

He was eighteen years old, naked under the California stars. The sky was ablaze. He felt he could reach for the stars and pluck them from the heavens.

To be a god. To possess the universe.

He turned to her. Her body was cool and slender, slightly tense. He cupped her breasts. He let his hand move across her flat belly. She shivered a little. "Dick," she said. "Oh." To be a god, he thought. He kissed her lightly, and then not lightly. "Wait," she said. "I'm not ready." He waited. He helped her get ready, or did the things he thought would help her get ready, and shortly she began to gasp. She spoke his name again. How many stars can a man visit in one lifetime? If each star has an average of twelve planets, and there are one hundred million stars within a galactic globe X light-years in diameter. . . . Her thighs opened. His eyes closed. He felt soft old pine needles against his knees and elbows. She was not his first, but the first that counted. As the lightning ripped through his brain he was dimly aware of her response, tentative, halting, then suddenly vigorous. The intensity of it frightened him, but only for a moment, and he rode with her to the end.

To be a god must be something like this.

They rolled over. He pointed to the stars and called off their names for her, getting half of them wrong, but she did not need to know that. He shared his dreams with her. Later they made love a second time, and it was even better.

He hoped it would rain at midnight, so they could dance in the rain, but the sky was clear. They went swimming instead, and came out shivering, laughing. When he took her home she washed down her pill with Chartreuse. He told her that he loved her.

They exchanged Christmas cards for several years.

3

The eighth world of Alpha Centauri B was a gas giant, with a low-density core and gravity not much more troublesome than that of Earth. Muller had honeymooned there the second time. It was partly a business trip, for there were troubles with the colonists on the sixth planet; they were talking of setting up a whirlpool effect that would suck away most of the eighth's world's highly useful atmosphere to use as raw materials.

Muller's conferences with the locals went fairly well. He persuaded them to accept a quota system for their atmospheric grabs, and even won their praise for the little lesson in interplanetary morality he had administered. Afterwards he and Nola were government guests for a holiday on the eighth world. Nola, unlike Lorayn, was the travelling sort. She would be accompanying him on many of his voyages.

Wearing support suits, they swam in an icy methane lake. They ran laughing along ammonia coasts. Nola was as tall as he, with powerful legs, dark red hair, green eyes. They embraced in a warm room of one-way windows overhanging a forlorn sea that stretched for hundreds of thousands of kilometres.

"For always," she said.

"Yes. For always."

Before the week ended they quarrelled bitterly. But it was only a game; for the more fiercely they quarrelled, the more passionate was the reconciliation. For a while. Later they stopped bothering to quarrel. When the option in the marriage contract came up, neither of them wanted to renew. Afterwards, as his reputation grew, he sometimes received friendly letters from her. He had tried to see her when he returned from Beta Hydri IV to Earth. Nola, he thought, would help him in his troubles. She of all people would not turn away from him. For old times' sake.

But she was vacationing on Vesta with her seventh husband. Muller found that out from her fifth husband. He had been her third. He did not call her. He began to see there was no point in it.

4

The surgeon said, "I'm sorry, Mr. Muller. There's nothing we can do for you. I wouldn't want to raise false hopes. We've graphed your whole neural network. We can't find the sites of alteration. I'm terribly sorry."

5

He had had nine years to sharpen his memories. He had filled a few cubes with reminiscences, but that had mainly been in the early years of his exile, when he worried about having his past drift away to be lost in fog. He discovered that the memories grew keener with age. Perhaps it was training. He could summon sights, sounds, tastes, odours. He could reconstruct whole conversations convincingly. He was able to quote the full texts of several treaties he had negotiated. He could name England's kings in sequence from first to last, William I through William VII. He remembered the names of the girls whose bodies he had known.

He admitted to himself that, given the chance, he would go back. Everything else had been pretence and bluster. He had fooled neither Ned Rawlins nor himself, he knew. The contempt he felt for mankind was real, but not the wish to remain isolated. He waited eagerly for Rawlins to return. While he waited he drank several goblets of the city's liqueur; he went on a killing spree, nervously gunning down animals he could not possibly consume in a year's time; he conducted intricate dialogues with himself; he dreamed of Earth.

6

Rawlins was running. Muller, standing a hundred metres deep in Zone C, saw him come striding through the entrance, breathless, flushed.

"You shouldn't run in here," Muller said, "not even in the safer zones. There's absolutely no telling—"

Rawlins sprawled down beside a flanged limestone tub, gripping its sides and sucking air. "Get me a drink, will

161

you?" he gasped. "That liqueur of yours—"

"Are you all right?"

"No."

Muller went to the fountain nearby and filled a handy flask with the sharp liqueur. Rawlins did not wince at all as Muller drew near to give it to him. He seemed altogether unaware of Muller's emanation. Greedily, sloppily, he emptied the flask, letting driblets of the gleaming fluid roll down his chin and on his clothes. Then he closed his eyes a moment.

"You look awful," Muller said. "As though you've just been raped, I'd say."

"I have."

"What's the trouble?"

"Wait. Let me get my breath. I ran all the way from Zone F."

"You're lucky to be alive, then."

"Perhaps."

"Another drink?"

"No," said Rawlins. "Not just yet."

Muller studied him, perplexed. The change was striking and unsettling, and mere fatigue could not account for it all. Rawlins was bloodshot, flushed, puffy-faced; his facial muscles were tightly knit; his eyes moved randomly, seeking and not finding. Drunk? Sick? Drugged?

Rawlins said nothing.

After a long moment Muller said, just to fill the vacuum of silence, "I've done a lot of thinking about our last conversation. I've decided that I was acting like a damned fool. All that cheap misanthropy I was dishing up." Muller knelt and tried to peer into the younger man's shifting eyes. "Look here, Ned, I want to take it all back. I'm willing to return to Earth for treatment. Even if the treatment's experimental, I'll chance it. I mean, the worst that can happen is that it won't cure me, and—"

"There's no treatment," said Rawlins dully.

"No—treatment . . ."

"No treatment. None. It was all a lie."

"Yes. Of course."

"You said so yourself," Rawlins reminded him. "You didn't believe a word of what I was saying. Remember?"

"A lie."

"You didn't understand why I was saying it, but you said it was nonsense. You told me I was lying. You wondered what I had to gain by lying. I *was* lying, Dick."

"Lying."

"Yes."

"But I've changed my mind," said Muller softly. "I was ready to go back to Earth."

"There's no hope of a cure," Rawlins told him.

He slowly rose to his feet and ran his hand through his long golden hair. He arranged his disarrayed clothing. He picked up the flask, went to the liqueur fountain and filled it. Returning, he handed the flask to Muller, who drank from it. Rawlins finished the flask. Something small and voracious-looking ran past them and slipped through the gate leading to Zone D.

Finally Muller said, "Do you want to explain some of this?"

"We aren't archaeologists."

"Go on."

"We came here looking especially for you. It wasn't any accident. We knew all along where you were. You were tracked from the time you left Earth nine years ago."

"I took precautions."

"They weren't any use. Boardman knew where you were going, and he had you tracked. He left you in peace because he had no use for you. But when a need developed he had to come after you. He was holding you in reserve, so to speak."

"Charles Boardman sent you to fetch me?" Muller asked.

"That's why we're here, yes. That's the whole purpose of this expedition," Rawlins replied tonelessly. "I was picked to make contact with you because you once knew my father and might trust me. And because I have an innocent face. All the time Boardman was directing me, telling me what to say, coaching me, even telling me what mistakes to make, how to blunder successfully. He told me to get into that cage, for instance. He thought it would help win your sympathy."

"Boardman is *here*? Here on Lemnos?"

"In Zone F. He's got a camp there."

"*Charles* Boardman?"

"He's here, yes. Yes."

Muller's face was stony. Within, all was turmoil. "Why did he do all this? What does he want with me?"

Rawlins said, "You know that there's a third intelligent race in the universe, beside us and the Hydrans."

"Yes. They had just been discovered when I left. That was why I went to visit the Hydrans. I was supposed to arrange a defensive alliance with them, before these other people, these extragalactics, came in contact with us. It didn't work. But what does this have to—"

"How much do you know about these extragalactics?"

"Very little," Muller admitted. "Essentially, nothing but what I've just told you. The day I agreed to go to Beta Hydri IV was the first time I had heard about them. Boardman told me, but he wouldn't say anything else. All he said was that they were extremely intelligent—a superior species, he said —and that they lived in a neighbouring cluster. And that they had a galactic drive and might visit us some day."

"We know more about them now," Rawlins said.

"First tell me what Boardman wants with me."

"Everything in order, and it'll be easier." Rawlins grinned, perhaps a bit tipsily. He leaned against the stone tub and stretched his legs far out in front of himself. He said, "We don't actually know a great deal about the extragalactics. What we did was send out a ramjet, throw it into warp, and bring it out a few thousand light-years away. Or a few million light-years. I don't know the details. Anyway, it was a drone ship with all sorts of eyes. The place it went to was one of the X-ray galaxies, classified information, but I've heard it was either in Cygnus A or Scorpius II. We found that one planet of the galactic system was inhabited by an advanced race of very alien aliens."

"How alien?"

"They can see all up and down the spectrum," Rawlins said. "Their basic visual range is in the high frequencies. They see by the light of X-rays. They also seem to be able to make use of the radio frequencies to see, or at least to get some kind of sensory information. And they pick up most wavelengths in between, except that they don't have a great deal of interest in the stuff between infra-red and ultra-violet. What we like to call the visible spectrum."

"Wait a minute. Radio senses? Do you have any idea how long radio waves are? If they're going to get any information out of a single wave, they'll need eyes or receptors or whatever of gigantic size. How big are these beings supposed to be?"

"They could eat elephants for breakfast," said Rawlins. "Intelligent life doesn't come that big."

"What's the limitation? This is a gas giant planet, all ocean, no gravity to speak of. They float. They have no square-cube problems."

"And a bunch of superwhales has developed a technological culture?" Muller asked. "You won't get me to believe—"

"They have," said Rawlins. "I've told you, these are very alien aliens. They can't build machinery themselves. But they have slaves."

"Oh," said Muller quietly.

"We're only beginning to understand this, and of course I don't have much of the inside information myself, but as I piece it together it seems that these beings make use of lower life-forms, turning them essentially into radio-controlled robots. They'll use anything with limbs and mobility. They started with certain animals of their own planet, a small dolphin-like form perhaps on the threshold of intelligence, and worked through them to achieve a space drive. Then they got to neighbouring planets—land planets—and took control of pseudoprimates, protochimps of some kind. They look for fingers. Manual dexterity counts a great deal with them. At present their sphere of influence covers some eighty light-years and appears to be spreading at an exponential rate."

Muller shook his head. "This is worse nonsense than the stuff you were handing me about a cure. Look, there's a limiting velocity for radio transmission, right? If they're controlling flunkeys from eighty light-years away, it'll take eighty years for any command to reach its destination. Every twitch of a muscle, every trifling movement—"

"They can leave their home world," said Rawlins.

"But if they're so big—"

"They've used their slave beings to build gravity tanks. They also have a star drive. All their colonies are run by overseers in orbit a few thousand kilometres up, floating in a simulated home-world environment. It takes one overseer to run one planet. I suppose they rotate tours of duty."

Muller closed his eyes a moment. The image came to him of these colossal, unimaginable beasts spreading through their distant galaxy, impressing animals of all sorts into service, forging a captive society, vicariously technological, and drifting in orbit like spaceborne whales to direct and co-ordinate the grandiose improbable enterprise while themselves remaining incapable of the smallest physical act. Monstrous masses of glossy pink protoplasm, fresh from the sea, bristling with perceptors functioning at both ends of the spectrum. Whispering to one another in pulses of X-rays. Sending out orders via radio. No, he thought. No.

"Well," he said at length, "what of it? They're in another galaxy."

"Not any longer. They've impinged on a few of our outlying colonies. Do you know what they do when they find a human world? They station an orbiting overseer above it and take control of the colonists. They find that humans make outstanding slaves, which isn't very surprising. At the moment they have six of our worlds. They had a seventh, but we shot up their overseer. Now they make it much harder to do that. They just take control of our missiles as they home in, and throw them back."

"If you're inventing this," said Muller, "I'll kill you!"

"It's true. I swear."

"When did this begin?"

"Within the past year."

"And what happens? Do they just march right through our galaxy and turn us all into zombies?"

"Boardman thinks we have one chance to prevent that."

"Which is?"

Rawlins said, "The aliens don't appear to realize that we're intelligent beings. We can't communicate with them, you see. They function on a completely nonverbal level, some kind of telepathic system. We've tried all sorts of ways to reach them, bombarding them with messages at every wavelength, without any flicker of a sign that they're receiving us. Boardman believes that if we could persuade them that we have—well, souls—they might leave us alone. God knows why he thinks so. It's some kind of computer prediction. He feels that these aliens work on a consistent moral scheme, that they're willing to grab any animals which look useful, but that they wouldn't touch a species that's on the same side of the intelligence boundary as they are. And if we could show them somehow—"

"They see that we have cities. That we have a star drive. Doesn't that prove intelligence?"

"Beavers make dams," said Rawlins. "But we don't make treaties with beavers. We don't pay reparations when we drain their marshes. We know that in some way a beaver's feelings don't count."

"Do we? Or have we simply decided arbitrarily that beavers are expendable? And what's this talk of an intelligence boundary? There's a continuous spectrum of intelligence, from the protozoa up through the primates. We're a little smarter than the chimps, sure, but is it a *qualitative* difference? Does the mere fact that we can record our knowledge and use it again make that much of a change?"

"I don't want to argue philosphy with you," Rawlins said hoarsely. "I'm trying to tell you what the situation is—and how it affects you."

"Yes. How it affects me."

"Boardman thinks that we really can get the radio beasts to leave our galaxy alone if we show them that we're closer to them in intelligence than we are to their other slaves. If we get across to them that we have emotions, needs, ambitions, dreams."

Muller spat. "Hath not a Jew eyes? Hath not a Jew hands, organs, dimensions, senses, affections, passions? If you prick us, do we not bleed?"

"Like that, yes."

"How do we get this across to them if they don't speak a verbal language?"

"Don't you see?" Rawlins asked.

"No, I—*yes*. Yes. God, yes!"

"We have one man, out of all our billions, who doesn't need words to communicate. He broadcasts his inner feelings. His soul. We don't know what frequency he uses, but *they* might."

"Yes. Yes."

"And so Boardman wanted to ask you to do one more thing for mankind. To go to these aliens. To allow them to pick up your broadcast. To show them what we are, that we're something more than beasts."

"Why the talk of taking me to Earth to be cured, then?"

"A trick. A trap. We had to get you out of the maze somehow. Once you were out, we could tell you the story and ask you to help."

"Admitting that there was no cure?"

"Yes."

"What makes you think I would lift a finger to keep all of man's worlds from being swallowed up?"

"Your help wouldn't have to be voluntary," Rawlins said.

7

Now it came flooding forth, the hatred, the anguish, the fear, the jealousy, the torment, the bitterness, the mockery, the loathing, the contempt, the despair, the viciousness, the fury, the desperation, the vehemence, the agitation, the grief, the pangs, the agony, the furor, the fire. Rawlins pulled back as though singed. Now Muller cruised the depths of desolation. A trick, a trick, all a trick! Used again. Boardman's tool. Muller blazed. He spoke only a few words aloud; the rest came from within, pouring out, the gates wide, nothing penned back, a torrent of anger.

When the wild spasm passed Muller said, standing braced between two jutting façades, "Boardman would dump me on to the aliens whether I was willing to go or not?"

"Yes. He said this was too important to allow you free choice. Your wishes are irrelevant. The many against the one."

With deadly calm Muller said, "You're part of this conspiracy. Why have you been telling me all this?"

"I resigned."

"Of course."

"No, I mean it. Oh, I was part of it. I was going along with Boardman, yes, I was lying in everything I said to you. But I didn't know the last part—that you wouldn't be given any choice. I had to pull out there. I couldn't let them do this to you. I had to tell you the truth."

"Very thoughtful. I now have two options, eh, Ned? I can let myself be dragged out of here to play catspaw for Boardman again—or I can kill myself a minute from now and let mankind go to hell. Yes?"

"Don't talk like that," Rawlins said edgily.

"Why not? Those are my options. You were kind enough to tell me the real situation, and now I can react as I choose. You've handed me a death sentence, Ned."

"No."

"What else is there? Let myself be used again?"

"You could—co-operate with Boardman," Rawlins said. He licked his lips. "I know it sounds crazy. But you could show him what you're made of. Forget all this bitterness. Turn the other cheek. Remember that Boardman isn't all of humanity. There are billions of innocent people—"

"Father, forgive them, for they know not what they do."

"Yes!"

"Every one of those billions would run from me if I came near."

"What of it? They can't help that! But they're your own people!"

"And I'm one of theirs. They didn't think of that when they cast me out."

"You aren't being rational."

"No I'm not. And I don't intend to start now. Assuming that it could affect humanity's destiny in the slightest if I became ambassador to these radio people—and I don't buy that idea at all—it would give me great pleasure to shirk my duty. I'm grateful to you for your warning. Now that at last I know what's going on here, I have the excuse I've been looking for all along. I know a thousand places here where death is quick and probably not painful. Then let Charles Boardman talk to the aliens himself. I—"

"Please don't move, Dick," said Boardman from a point about thirty metres behind him.

CHAPTER TWELVE

BOARDMAN FOUND all this distasteful. But it was also necessary, and he was not surprised that events had taken this turn. In his original analysis he had forecast two events of equal probability : that Rawlins would succeed in winning Muller out of the maze, and that Rawlins would ultimately rebel and blurt out the truth. He was prepared for either.

Now Boardman had advanced into the centre of the maze, coming from Zone F to follow Rawlins before the damage became irreparable. He could predict one of Muller's likely responses : suicide. Muller would never commit suicide out of despair, but he might do it by way of vengeance. With Boardman were Ottavio, Davis, Reynolds, and Greenfield. Hosteen and the others were monitoring from outer zones. All were armed.

Muller turned. The look on his face was not easy to behold.

"I'm sorry, Dick," Boardman said. "We had to do this."

"You have no shame at all, do you?" Muller asked.

"Not where Earth is concerned."

"I realized that a long time ago. But I thought you were human, Charles. I didn't comprehend your depths."

"I wish we didn't have to do any of this, Dick. But we do. Come with us."

"No."

"You can't refuse. The boy's told you what's at stake. We already owe you more than we can ever repay, Dick, but run the debt a little higher. Please."

"I'm not leaving Lemnos. I feel no sense of obligation to humanity. I won't do your work."

"Dick—"

Muller said, "Fifty metres to the northwest of where I stand is a flame pit. I'm going to walk over and step into it. Within ten seconds there will be no more Richard Muller. One unfortunate calamity will cancel out another, and

Earth will be no worse off than it was before I acquired my special ability. Since you people didn't appreciate that ability before, I can't see any reason for letting you make use of it now."

"If you want to kill yourself," Boardman said, "why not wait a few months?"

"Because I don't care to be of service."

"That's childish. The last sin I'd ever imagine *you* committing."

"It was childish of me to dream of stars," Muller said. "I'm simply being consistent. The galactics can eat you alive, Charles. I don't care if they do. Won't you fancy being a slave? Somewhere under your skull you'll still be there, screaming to be released, and the radio messages will tell you which arm to lift, which leg to move. I wish I could last long enough to see that. But I'm going to walk into that flame pit. Do you want to wish me a good journey? Come close, let me touch your arm. Get a good dose of me first. Your last. I'll cease to give offence." Muller was trembling. His face was sweaty. His upper lip quivered.

Boardman said, "At least come out to Zone F with me. Let's sit down quietly and discuss this over brandy."

"Side by side?" Muller laughed. "You'd vomit. You couldn't bear it."

"I'm willing to talk."

"I'm not," Muller said. He took a shaky step towards the northwest. His big powerful body seemed shrunken and withered, nothing but sinews stretching tighter over a yielding armature. He took another step. Boardman watched. Ottavio and Davis stood beside him to the left; Reynolds and Greenfield on the other side, between Muller and the flame pit. Rawlins, like an afterthought, was alone at the far side of the group.

Boardman felt a throbbing in his larynx, a stirring and a tickle of tension in his loins. A great weariness possessed him and at the same time a fierce soaring excitement of a kind he had not known since he had been a young man. He allowed Muller to take a third step towards self-destruction. Then casually, Boardman gestured with two flicking fingers.

172

Greenfield and Reynolds pounced.

Catlike they darted forth, ready for this, and caught Muller by the inner forearms. Boardman saw the greyness sweep over their faces as the impact of Muller's field got to them. Muller struggled, heaved, tried to break loose. Davis and Ottavio were upon him now too. In the gathering darkness the group formed a surging Laocoon, Muller only half visible as the smaller men coiled and wound about his flexed battling body. A stungun would have been easier, Boardman reflected. But stunguns were risky, sometimes, on humans. They had been known to send hearts into wild runaways. They had no defibrillator here.

A moment more, and Muller was forced to his knees.

"Disarm him," Boardman said.

Ottavio and Davis held him. Reynolds and Greenfield searched him. From a pocket Greenfield pulled forth the deadly little windowed globe. "That's all he seems to be carrying," Greenfield said.

"Check carefully."

They checked. Meanwhile Muller remained motionless, his face frozen, his eyes stony. It was the posture and the expression of a man at the headsman's block. At length Greenfield looked up again. "Nothing," he said.

Muller said, "One of my left upper molars contains a secret compartment full of carniphage. I'll count to ten and bite hard, and I'll melt away before your eyes."

Greenfield swung around and grabbed for Muller's jaws.

Boardman said, "Leave him alone. He's joking."

"But how do we know—" Greenfield began.

"Let him be. Step back." Boardman gestured. "Stand five metres away from him. Don't go near him unless he moves."

They stepped away, obviously grateful to get back from the full thrust of Muller's field. Boardman, fifteen metres from him, could feel faint strands of pain. He went no closer.

"You can stand up now," Boardman said. "But please don't try to move. I regret this, Dick."

Muller got to his feet. His face was black with hatred. But he said nothing, nor did he move.

"If we have to," Boardman said, "we'll tape you in a webfoam cradle and carry you out of the maze to the ship. We'll keep you in foam from then on. You'll be in foam when you meet the aliens. You'll be absolutely helpless. I would hate to do that to you, Dick. The other choice is willing co-operation. Go with us of your own free will to the ship. Do what we ask of you. Help us this last time."

"May your intestines rust," said Muller almost casually. "May you live a thousand years with worms eating you. May you choke on your own smugness and never die."

"Help us. Willingly."

"Put me in the webfoam, Charles. Otherwise I'll kill myself the first chance I get."

"What a villain I must seem, eh?" Boardman said. "But I don't want to do it this way. Come willingly, Dick."

Muller's reply was close to a snarl.

Boardman sighed. This was an embarrassment. He looked towards Ottavio.

"The webfoam," he said.

Rawlins, who had been standing as though in a trance, burst into sudden activity. He darted forward, seized Reynolds' gun from its holster, ran towards Muller and pressed the weapon into his hand. "There," he said thickly. "Now you're in charge!"

2

Muller studied the gun as though he had never seen one before, but his surprise lasted only a fraction of a second. He slipped his hand around its comfortable butt and fingered the firing stud. It was a familiar model, only slightly changed from those he had known. In a quick flaring burst he could kill them all. Or himself. He stepped back so they could not come upon him from the rear. Probing with his kickstaff, he checked the wall, found it trustworthy, and planted his shoulderblades against it. Then he moved the gun in an arc of some 270°, taking them all in.

"Stand close together," he said. "The six of you. Stand one metre apart in a straight row, and keep your hands out where I can see them at all times."

He enjoyed the black, glowering look that Boardman threw at Ned Rawlins. The boy seemed dazed, flushed, confused, a figure in a dream. Muller waited patiently as the six men arranged themselves according to his orders. He was surprised at his own calmness.

"You look unhappy, Charles," he said. "How old are you now, eighty years? You'd like to live that other seventy, eighty, ninety, I guess. You have your career planned, and the plan doesn't include dying on Lemnos. Stand still, Charles. And stand straight. You won't win any pity from me by trying to look old and sagging. I know that dodge. You're as healthy as I am, beneath the phony flab. Healthier. Straight, Charles!"

Boardman said raggedly, "If it'll make you feel better, Dick, kill me. And then go aboard the ship and do what we want you to do. I'm expendable."

"Do you mean that?"

"Yes."

"I almost think you do," Muller said wonderingly. "You crafty old bastard, you're offering a trade! Your life for my co-operation! But where's the *quid pro quo*? I don't enjoy killing. It won't soothe me at all to burn you down. I'll still have my curse."

"The offer stands."

"Rejected," Muller said. "If I kill you, it won't be as part of any deal. But I'm much more likely to kill myself. You know, I'm a decent man at heart. Somewhat unstable, yes, and who's to blame me for that? But decent. I'd rather use this gun on me than on you. I'm the one who's suffering. I can end it."

"You could have ended it at any time in the past nine years," Boardman pointed out. "But you survived. You devoted all your ingenuity to staying alive in this murderous place."

"Ah. Yes. But that was different! An abstract challenge, man against the maze. A test of my skills. Ingenuity. But if I kill myself now, I thwart you. I put the thumb to the nose, with all of mankind watching. I'm the indispensable man, you say? What better way then, to pay mankind back for my pain?"

"We regretted your suffering," said Boardman.

"I'm sure you wept bitterly for me. But that was all you did. You let me go creeping away, diseased, corrupt, unclean. Now comes the release. Not really suicide, but revenge." Muller smiled. He turned the gun to finest beam and let its muzzle rest against his chest. A touch of the finger, now. His eyes raked their faces. The four soldiers did not seem to care. Rawlins appeared deep in shock. Only Boardman was animated with concern and fright. "I could kill you first, I suppose, Charles. As a lesson to our young friend—the wages of deceit is death. But no. That would spoil everything. You have to live, Charles. To go back to earth and admit that you let the indispensable man slip through your grasp. What a blotch on your career! To fail your most important assignment! Yes. Yes. My pleasure. Falling dead here, leaving you to pick up the pieces."

His finger tightened on the stud.

"Now," he said. "Quickly."

"No!" Boardman screamed. "For the love of—"

"Man," said Muller, and laughed, and did not fire. His arm relaxed. He tossed the weapon contemptuously towards Boardman. It landed almost at his feet.

"Foam!" Boardman cried. "Quick!"

"Don't bother," said Muller. "I'm yours."

3

Rawlins took a long while to understand it. First they had the problem of getting out of the maze. Even with Muller as their leader, it was a taxing job. As they had suspected, coming upon the traps from the inner side was not the same as working through them from without. Warily Muller took them through Zone E; they could manage F well enough by now; and after they had dismantled their camp, they pressed on into G. Rawlins kept expecting Muller to bolt suddenly and hurl himself into some fearful snare. But he seemed as eager to come alive out of the maze as any of them. Boardman, oddly, appeared to recognize that. Though he watched

Muller closely, he left him unconfined.

Feeling that he was in disgrace, Rawlins kept away from the others on the nearly silent outward march. He considered his career in ruins. He had jeopardized the lives of his companions and the success of the mission. Yet it had been worth it, he felt. A time comes when a man takes his stand against what he believes to be wrong.

The simple moral pleasure that he took in that was balanced and overbalanced by the knowledge that he had acted naïvely, romantically, foolishly. He could not bear to face Boardman now. He thought more than once of letting one of the deadly traps of these outer zones have him; but that too, he decided, would be naïve, romantic, and foolish.

He watched Muller striding ahead—tall, proud, all tensions resolved, all doubts crystallized. And he wondered a thousand times why Muller had given back the gun.

Boardman finally explained to him when they camped for the night in a precarious plaza near the outward side of Zone G.

"Look at me," Boardman said. "What's the matter? Why can't you look at me?"

"Don't toy with me, Charles. Get it over with."

"Get what over with?"

"The tonguelashing. The sentence."

"It's all right, Ned. You helped us get what we wanted. Why should I be angry?"

"But the gun—I gave him the gun—"

"Confusion of ends and means again. He's coming with us. He's doing what we wanted him to do. That's what counts."

Floundering, Rawlins asked, "And if he had killed himself—or us?"

"He wouldn't have done either."

"You can say that, now. But for the first moment, when he held the gun—"

"No," Boardman said. "I told you earlier, we'd work on his sense of honour. Which we had to reawaken. You did that. Look, here I am, the brutal agent of a brutal and amoral society, right? And I confirm all of Muller's worst thoughts about mankind. Why should he help a tribe of wolves? And here you are, young and innocent, full of hope and dreams. You remind him of the mankind he once served, before the cynicism corroded him. In your blundering way you try to be moral in a world that shows no trace of morality or meaning. You demonstrate sympathy, love for a fellow man, the willingness to make a dramatic gesture for the sake of righteousness. You show Muller that there's still hope in humanity. See? You defy me, and give him a gun and make him master of the situation. He could do the obvious, and burn us down. He could do the slightly less obvious, and burn himself. Or he could match your gesture with one of his own, top it, commit a deliberate act of renunciation, express his revived sense of moral superiority. He does it. He tosses away the gun. You were vital, Ned. You were the instrument through which we won him."

"You make it sound so ugly when you spell it out that way, Charles. As if you had planned even this. Pushing me so far that I'd give him the gun, knowing that he—"

Boardman smiled.

"Did you?" Rawlins demanded suddenly. "No. You couldn't have calculated all those twists and turns. Now, after the fact, you're trying to claim credit for having engineered it all. But I saw you in the moment I handed him the gun. There was fear on your face, and anger. You weren't at all sure what he was going to do. Only when everything worked out could you claim it went according to plan. I see through you, Charles!"

"How delightful to be transparent," Boardman said gaily.

4

The maze seemed uninterested in holding them. Carefully they traced their outward path, but they met few challenges and no serious dangers. Quickly they went towards the ship.

They gave Muller a forward cabin, well apart from the quarters of the crew. He seemed to accept that as a necessity of his condition, and showed no offence. He was withdrawn, subdued, self-contained; an ironic smile often played on his lips, and much of the time his eyes displayed a glint of contempt. But he was willing to do as they directed. He had had his moment of supremacy; now he was theirs.

Hosteen and his men bustled through the liftoff preparations. Muller remained in his cabin. Boardman went to him, alone, unarmed. He could make noble gestures too.

They faced each other across a low table. Muller waited, silent, his face cleansed of emotion. Boardman said after a long moment, "I'm grateful to you, Dick."

"Save it."

"I don't mind if you despise me. I did what I had to do. So did the boy. And now so will you. You couldn't forget that you were an Earthman, after all."

"I wish I could."

"Don't say that. It's easy, glib, cheap bitterness, Dick. We're both too old for glibness. The universe is a perilous place. We do our best. Everything else is unimportant."

He sat quite close to Muller. The emanation hit him broadside, but he deliberately remained in place. That wave of despair welling out to him made him feel a thousand years old. The decay of the body, the crumbling of the soul, the heat-death of the galaxy . . . the coming of winter . . . emptiness . . . ashes . . .

"When we reach Earth," said Boardman crisply, "I'll put you through a detailed briefing. You'll come out of it knowing as much about the radio people as we do, which isn't saying a great deal. After that you'll be on your own. But I'm sure you'll realize, Dick, that the hearts and souls of billions of Earthmen will be praying for your success and safety."

"Who's being glib now?" Muller asked.

"Is there anyone you'd like me to have waiting for you when we dock Earthside?"

"No."

"I can send word ahead. There are people who've never stopped loving you, Dick. They'll be there if I ask them."

Muller said slowly, "I see the strain in your eyes, Charles. You feel the nearness of me, and it's ripping you apart. You feel it in your gut. In your forehead. Back of your breastbone. Your face is going grey. Your cheeks are sagging. You'll sit here if it kills you, yes, because that's your style. But it's hell for you. If there's anyone on Earth who never stopped loving me, Charles, the least I can do is spare her from hell. I don't want to meet anyone. I don't want to see anyone. I don't want to talk to anyone."

"As you wish," said Boardman. Beads of sweat hung from his bushy brows and dropped to his cheeks. "Perhaps you'll change your mind when you're close to Earth."

"I'll never be close to Earth again," Muller said.

CHAPTER THIRTEEN

HE SPENT three weeks absorbing all that was known of the giant extragalactic beings. At his insistence he did not set foot on Earth during that time, nor was his return from Lemnos made known to the public. They gave him quarters in a bunker on Luna and he lived quietly beneath Copernicus, moving like a robot through steely grey corridors lit by warm glowing torches. They showed him all the cubes. They ran off a variety of reconstructs in every sensory mode. Muller listened. He absorbed. He said very little.

They kept well away from him, as they had on the voyage from Lemnos. Whole days passed in which he saw no human being. When they came to him they remained at a distance of ten metres and more.

He did not object.

The exception was Boardman, who visited him three times a week and made a point always of coming well within the pain range. Muller found that contemptible. Boardman seemed to be patronizing him with his voluntary and wholly unnecessary submission to discomfort. "I wish you'd keep away," Muller told him on the fifth visit. "We can talk by screen. Or you could stay by the door."

"I don't mind the close contact."

"I do," said Muller. "Has it ever occurred to you that I've begun to find mankind as odious as mankind finds me? The reek of your meaty body, Charles—it goes into my nostrils like a spike. Not just you; all the others too. Sickening. Hideous. Even the look of your faces. The pores. The stupid gaping mouths. The ears. Look at a human ear closely some time, Charles. Have you ever seen anything more repulsive than that pink wrinkled cup? You all disgust me!"

"I'm sorry you feel that way," Boardman said.

The briefing went on and on. Muller was ready after the first week to undertake his assignment, but no, first they had to feed him all the data in the bank. He absorbed the information with twitchy impatience. A shadow of his old self remained to find it fascinating, a challenge worth accepting. He would go. He would serve as before. He would honour his obligation.

At last they said he could depart.

From Luna they took him by iondrive to a point outside the orbit of Mars, where they transferred him to a warp-drive ship already programmed to kick him to the edge of the galaxy. Alone. He would not, on this voyage, have to take care not to distress the crew by his presence. There were several reasons for this, the most important being that the mission was officially considered close to suicidal; and, since a ship could make the voyage without the use of a crew, it would have been rash to risk lives—other than his, of course. But he was a volunteer. Besides, Muller had requested a solo flight.

He did not see Boardman during the five days prior to his departure, nor had he seen Ned Rawlins at all since their return from Lemnos. Muller did not regret the absence of Boardman, but he sometimes wished he could have another hour with Rawlins. There was promise in that boy. Behind all the confusion and the foggy innocence, Muller thought, lay the seeds of manhood.

From the cabin of his small sleek ship he watched the technicians drifting in space, getting ready to sever the transfer line. Then they were returning to their own ship. Now he heard from Boardman, a final message, a Boardman special, inspirational, go forth and do your duty for mankind, et cetera, et cetera. Muller thanked him graciously for his words.

The communications channel was cut.

Moments later Muller entered warp.

2

The aliens had taken possession of three solar systems on the fringes of the galactic lens, each star having two Earth-settled planets. Muller's ship was aimed at a greenish-gold star whose worlds had been colonized only forty years before.

The fifth planet, dry as iron, belonged to a Central Asian colonization society which was trying to establish a series of pastoral cultures where nomad virtues could be practised. The sixth, with a more typically Earth-like mixture of climates and environments, was occupied by representatives of half a dozen colonization societies, each on its own continent. The relations between these groups, often intricate and touchy, had ceased to matter within the past twelve months, for both planets now were under control of extragalactic overseers.

Muller emerged from warp twenty light-seconds from the sixth planet. His ship automatically went into an observation orbit, and the scanners began to report. Screens showed him the surface picture; via template overlay he was able to compare the configurations of the outposts below with the pattern as it had been prior to alien conquest. The amplified images were quite interesting. The original settlements appeared on his screen in violet, and the recent extensions in red. Muller observed that about each of the colonies, regardless of its original ground plan, there had sprouted a network of angular streets and jagged avenues. Instinctively he recognized the geometries as alien. There sprang to mind the vivid memory of the maze; and though the patterns here bore no resemblance to those of the maze, they were alike in their lack of recognizable symmetries. He rejected the possibility that the labyrinth of Lemnos had been built long ago by direction of the radio beings. What he saw here was only the similarity of total difference. Aliens built in alien ways.

In orbit, seven thousand kilometres above the sixth planet, was a glistening capsule, slightly longer on one axis than on the other, which had about the mass of a large interstellar transport ship. Muller found a similar capsule in orbit about the fifth world. The overseers.

It was impossible for him to open communications with either of these capsules or with the planets beyond. All channels were blocked. He twisted dials fitfully for more than an hour, ignoring the irritable responses of the ship's brain which kept telling him to give up the idea. At last he conceded.

He brought his ship close to the nearer orbiting capsule.

To his surprise the ship remained under his control. Destructive missiles that had come this close to alien overseers had been commandeered, but he was able to navigate. A hopeful sign? Was he under scan, and was the alien able to distinguish him from a hostile weapon? Or was he being ignored?

At a distance of one million kilometres he matched velocities with the alien satellite and put his ship in a parking orbit around it. He entered his drop-capsule. He ejected himself and slid from his ship into darkness.

3

Now the alien seized him. There was no doubt. The drop-capsule was programmed for a minimum-expenditure orbit that would bring it skimming past the alien in due time, but Muller swiftly discovered that he was deviating from that orbit. Deviations are never accidental. His capsule was accelerating beyond the programme, which meant that it had been grasped and was being drawn forward. He accepted that. He was icily calm, expecting nothing and prepared for everything. The drop-capsule eased down. He saw the gleaming bulk of the alien satellite now.

Skin to metal skin, the vehicles met and touched and joined.

A hatch slid open.

He drifted within.

His capsule came to rest on a board platform in an immense cavernous room hundreds of metres long, high, and broad. Fully suited, Muller stepped from it. He activated his gravity pads; for, as he had anticipated, gravity in here was so close to null that the pull was imperceptible. In the blackness he saw only a faint purplish glow. Against a backdrop of utter silence he heard a resonant booming sound, like an enormously amplified sigh, shuddering through the struts and trusses of the satellite. Despite his gravity pads he felt dizzy; beneath him the floor rolled. Through his mind went a sensation like the throbbing of the sea; great waves slammed against ragged beaches; a mass of water stirred and groaned in its global cavity; the world shivered beneath the burden. Muller felt a chill that his suit could not counteract. An irresistible force drew him. Hesitantly he moved, relieved and surprised to see that his limbs still obeyed his commands though he was not entirely their master. The awareness of something vast nearby, something heaving and pulsating and sighing, remained with him.

He walked down a night-drowned boulevard. He came to a low railing—a dull red line against the deep darkness—and pressed his leg against it, keeping contact with it as he moved forward. At one point he slipped and as he hit the railing with his elbow he heard the clang of metal travelling through the entire structure. Blurred echoes drifted back to him. As though walking the maze he passed through corridors and hatches, across interlocking compartments, over bridges that spanned dark abysses, down sloping ramplike debouchments into lofty chambers whose ceilings were dimly visible. Here he moved in blind confidence, fearing nothing. He could barely see. He had no vision of the total structure of this satellite. He could scarcely imagine the purpose of these inner partitions.

From that hidden giant presence came silent waves, an ever-intensifying pressure. He trembled in its grip. Still he moved on, until now he was in some central gallery, and by a thin blue glow he was able to discern levels dwindling below him, and far beneath his balcony a broad tank, and within the tank something sparkling, something huge.

"Here I am," he said. "Richard Muller. Earthman."

He gripped the railing and peered downward, expecting anything. Did the great beast stir and shift? Did it grunt? Did it call to him in a language he understood? He heard nothing. But he felt a great deal : slowly, subtly, he became aware of a contact, of a mingling, of an engulfment.

He felt his soul escaping through his pores.

The drain was unrelenting. Yet Muller chose not to resist; he yielded, he welcomed, he gave freely. Down in the pit the monster tapped his spirit, opened petcocks of neural energy, drew forth from him, demanded more, drew that too.

"Go on," Muller said, and the echoes of his voice danced

around him, chiming, reverberating. "Drink! What's it like? A bitter brew, eh? Drink! Drink!" His knees buckled, and he sagged forward, and he pressed his forehead to the cold railing as his last reservoirs were plumbed.

He surrendered himself gladly, in glittering droplets. He gave up first love and first disappointment, April rain, fever and ache. Pride and hope, warmth and cold, sweet and sour. The scent of sweat and the touch of flesh, the thunder of music, the music of thunder, silken hair knotted between his fingers, lines scratched in spongy soil. Snorting stallions; glittering schools of tiny fish; the towers of Newer Chicago; the brothels of Under New Orleans. Snow. Milk. Wine. Hunger. Fire. Pain. Sleep. Sorrow. Apples. Dawn. Tears. Bach. Sizzling grease. The laughter of old men. The sun on the horizon, the moon on the sea, the light of other stars, the fumes of rocket fuel, summer flowers on a glacier's flank. Father. Mother. Jesus. Mornings. Sadness. Joy. He gave it all, and much more, and he waited for an answer. None came to him. And when he was wholly empty he lay face downward, drained, hollow, staring blindly into the abyss.

4

When he was able to leave, he left. The hatch opened to pass his drop-capsule, and it rose towards his ship. Shortly he was in warp. He slept most of the way. In the vicinity of Antares he cut in the override, took command of the ship, and filed for a change of course. There was no need to return to Earth. The monitor station recorded his request, checked routinely to see that the channel was clear, and allowed him to proceed at once to Lemnos. Muller entered a warp again instantly.

When he emerged, not far from Lemnos, he found another ship already in orbit and waiting for him. He started to go about his business anyway, but the other ship insisted on making contact. Muller accepted the communication.

"This is Ned Rawlins," a strangely quiet voice said. "Why have you changed your flight plan?"

"Does it matter? I've done my job."

"You haven't filed a report."

"I'm reporting now, then. I visited the alien. We had a pleasant, friendly chat. Then it let me go home. Now I'm almost home. I don't know what effect my visit will have on the future of human history. End of report."

"What are you going to do now?"

"Go home, I said. This is home."

"Lemnos?"

"Lemnos."

"Dick, let me come aboard. Give me ten minutes with you—in person. Please don't say no."

"I don't say no," Muller replied.

Soon a small craft detached itself from the other ship and matched velocities with his. Patiently, Muller allowed the rendezvous to take place. Rawlins stepped into his ship and shed his helmet. He looked pale, drawn, older. His eyes held a different expression. They faced one another for a long silent moment. Rawlins advanced and took Muller's wrist in greeting.

"I never thought I'd see you again, Dick," he began. "And I wanted to tell you—"

He stopped abruptly.

"Yes?" Muller asked.

"I don't feel it," said Rawlins. "*I don't feel it!*"

"What?"

"You. Your field. Look, I'm right next to you. I don't feel a thing. All that nastiness, the pain, the despair—it isn't coming through!"

"The alien drank it all," said Muller calmly. "I'm not surprised. My soul left my body. Not all of it was put back."

"What are you talking about?"

"I could feel it soaking up everything that was within me. I knew it was changing me. Not deliberately. It was just an incidental alteration. A byproduct."

Rawlins said slowly, "You knew it, then. Even before I came on board."

"This confirms it, though."

"And yet you want to return to the maze. Why?"

"It's home."

"Earth's your home, Dick. There's no reason why you shouldn't go back. You've been cured."

"Yes," said Muller. "A happy ending to my doleful story. I'm fit to consort with humanity again. My reward for nobly risking my life a second time among aliens. How neatly done! But is humanity fit to consort with me?"

"Don't go down there, Dick. You're being irrational now. Charles sent me to get you. He's terribly proud of you. We all are. It would be a big mistake to lock yourself away in the maze now."

"Go back to your own ship, Ned," Muller said.

"If you go into the maze, so will I."

"I'll kill you if you do. I want to be left alone, Ned, do you understand that? I've done my job. My last job. Now I retire, purged of my nightmares." Muller forced a thin smile. "Don't come after me, Ned. I trusted you, and you would have betrayed me. Everything else is incidental. Leave my ship now. We've said all that we need to say to each other, I think, except goodbye."

"Dick—"

"Goodbye, Ned. Remember me to Charles. And to all the others."

"Don't do this!"

"There's something down there I don't want to lose," Muller said. "I'm going to claim it now. Stay away. All of you. Stay away. I've learned the truth about Earthmen. Will you go now?"

Silently Rawlins suited up. He moved towards the hatch. As he stepped through it, Muller said, "Say goodbye to all of them for me, Ned. I'm glad you were the last one I saw. Somehow it was easier that way."

Rawlins vanished through the hatch.

A short while later Muller programmed his ship for a hyperbolic orbit on a twenty-minute delay, got into his drop capsule, and readied himself for the descent to Lemnos. It was a quick drop and a good landing. He came down right in the impact area, two kilometres from the gateway to the maze. The sun was high and bright. Muller walked briskly towards the maze.

He had done what they wanted him to do.

Now he was going home.

5

"He's still making gestures," Boardman said. "He'll come out of there."

"I don't think so," replied Rawlins. "He meant that."

"You stood next to him, and you felt nothing?"

"Nothing. He doesn't have it any more."

"Which he realizes?"

"Yes."

"He'll come out, then," Boardman said. "We'll watch him, and when he asks to be taken off Lemnos, we'll take him off. Sooner or later he'll need other people again. He's been through so much that he needs to think everything through, and I guess he sees the maze as the best place for that. He isn't ready to plunge back into normal life again. Give him two years, three, four. He'll come out. The two sets of aliens have cancelled each other's work on him, and he's fit to rejoin society."

"I don't think so," Rawlins said quietly. "I don't think it cancelled out so evenly. Charles, I don't think he's human at all—any more."

Boardman laughed. "Shall we bet? I'll offer five to one that Muller comes out of the maze voluntarily within five years."

"Well—"

"It's a bet, then."

Rawlins left the older man's office. Night had fallen. He crossed the bridge outside the building. In an hour he'd be dining with someone warm and soft and willing, who was awed beyond measure by her liaison with the famous Ned Rawlins. She was a good listener, who coaxed him for tales of daring deeds and nodded gravely as he spoke of the challenges ahead. She was also good in bed.

He paused on the bridge to look upward at the stars.

A million million blazing points of light shimmered in the sky. Out there lay Lemnos, and Beta Hydri IV, and the world's occupied by the radio beings, and all man's dominion, and even, invisible but real, the home galaxy of the others. Out there lay a labyrinth in a broad plain, and a forest of spongy trees hundreds of metres high, and a thousand planets planted with the young cities of Earthmen, and a tank of strangeness orbiting a conquered world. In the tank lay something unbearably alien. On the thousand planets lived worried men fearing the future. Under the spongy trees walked graceful silent creatures with many arms. In the maze dwelled a . . . man.

Perhaps, Rawlins thought, I'll visit Muller in a year or two.

It was too early to tell how the patterns would form. No one yet knew how the radio people were reacting, if at all, to the things they had learned from Richard Muller. The role of the Hydrans, the efforts of men in their own defence, the coming forth of Muller from the maze, these were mysteries —shifting, variable. It was exciting and a little frightening to think that he would live through the time of testing that lay ahead.

He crossed the bridge. He watched starships shattering the darkness overhead. He stood motionless, feeling the pull of the stars. All the universe tugged at him, each star exerting its finite power. The glow of the heavens dazzled him. Beckoning pathways lay open. He thought of the man in the maze. He thought too of the girl, lithe and passionate, dark-eyed, her eyes mirrors of silver, her body awaiting him.

Suddenly he was Dick Muller, once also twenty-four years old, with the galaxy his for the asking. Was it any different for you, he wondered? What did you feel when you looked up at the stars? Where did it hit you? Here. Here. Just where it hits me. And you went out there. And found. And lost. And found something else. Do you remember, Dick, the way you once felt? Tonight in your windy maze, what will you think about? Will you remember?

Why did you turn away from us, Dick?

What have you become?

He hurried to the girl who waited for him. They sipped young wine, tart, electric. They smiled through a candle' flickering glow. Later her softness yielded to him, and stil

190

later they stood close together on a balcony looking out over the greatest of all man's cities. Lights stretched towards infinity, rising to meet those other lights above. He slipped his arm around her, put his hand on her bare flank, held her against him.

She said. "How long do you stay this time?"

"Four more days."

"And when will you come back?"

"When the job's done."

"Ned, will you ever rest? Will you ever say you've had enough, that you won't go out any longer, that you'll take one planet and stick to it?"

"Yes," he said vaguely. "I suppose. After a while."

"You don't mean it. You're just saying it. None of you ever settle down."

"We can't," he murmured. "We keep going. There are always more worlds . . . new suns. . . ."

"You want too much. You want the whole universe. It's a sin, Ned. You have to accept limits."

"Yes," he said. "You're right. I know you're right." His fingers travelled over satin-smooth flesh. She trembled. He said, "We do what we have to do. We try to learn from the mistakes of others. We serve our cause. We attempt to be honest with ourselves. How else can it be?"

"The man who went back into the maze—"

"—is happy," Rawlins said. "He's following his chosen course."

"How can that be?"

"I can't explain."

"He must hate us all terribly to turn his back on the whole universe like that."

"He's beyond hate," Rawlins said. "Somehow. He's at peace. Whatever he is."

"*Whatever?*"

"Yes," he said gently. He felt the midnight chill and led her inside. They stood by the bed. The candle was nearly out. He kissed her solemnly, and thought of Dick Muller again, and wondered what maze was waiting for him at the end of his own path. He drew her into his arms and felt the impress of hardening flesh against his own cool skin. They lowered themselves. His hands sought, grasped, caressed. Her breath grew ragged.

When I see you again, Dick, I have much to tell you, he thought.

She said, "Why did he lock himself into the maze again, Ned?"

"For the same reason that he went among aliens in the first place. For the reason that it all happened."

"And that reason was?"

"He loved mankind." Rawlins said. It was as good an epitaph as any. He held the girl tightly. But he left before dawn.